Shouts and Whispers

Stories from the Southern Chesapeake Bay

Best Wishes

Jim Charbeneau

Shouts and Whispers

Stories from the Southern Chesapeake Bay

Jim Charbeneau

Illustrations by J. T. Carver

BRANDYLANE PUBLISHERS
WHITE STONE, VIRGINIA

 BRANDYLANE PUBLISHERS

P.O. Box 261, White Stone, Virginia 22578

(804) 435-6900 or 1 800 553-6922; e-mail: brandy@crosslink.net

Library of Congress Cataloging-in-Publication Data

Charbeneau, Jim, 1936–
    Shouts and whispers: stories from the southern Chesapeake Bay/Jim
    Charbeneau.
        p.   cm.
    ISBN 1-883911-11-7
    1. Chesapeake Bay (Md. and Va.)—Fiction. I. Title.
PS3553.H317S48   1997
813'.54—dc20   96-43891
                                                                      CIP

Dedication

To Roland and Mary, for a lifetime of encouragement and parental love.

Contents

Acknowledgments

Thanks to Hanne Caraher who reviewed the first of my short stories and still encouraged me to continue writing. To Robert Pruett who published the first of the stories, *Outrageous*, in *Pleasant Living* magazine and edited and published this book, and to Suzanne Best who typed, proofed and formatted it for publication.

Thanks to Dave McCarty and J. T. Carver for the beautiful cover work. The chart depicted on the cover was extracted from an 1856 Coast and Geodetic Survey chart and modified to include, among other things, Bayberry Creek. Thanks also to J. T. for the illustrations contained herein, and for his insightful criticism of story endings.

Special thanks to Carol, my severest critic, proofreader extraordinaire, good friend and patient wife.

Introduction

The fourteen stories in this book were written in a two-year period from mid-1994 to mid-1996, shortly after my wife and I had moved to Virginia's Northern Neck. The Northern Neck is a peninsula, situated between the Potomac River on the north, the Rappahannock River on the south, and Chesapeake Bay on the east. The birthplace of both George Washington and Robert E. Lee, it is an area of great historic significance and natural beauty. The land is deeply incised by dozens of rivers and creeks, and fishing, crabbing, and oystering from these waters and the Bay are still principal sources of employment. No railroads run down the peninsula and until the middle of the 1920s no bridges crossed the lower parts of its great rivers. Indeed, from the mid-1800s until the 1930s the lower end of the peninsula was reached primarily by steamboat.

The Neck and its traditional ways of life are changing, although more slowly than many formerly isolated East Coast areas. The natural resources of the Chesapeake Bay and the large rivers which feed it are being depleted, and each year fewer watermen are able to support their families in the crabbing and oystering industry. During recent years, retirees from urban centers have discovered the beauty of this peninsula and the slower-paced life and recreational opportunities it offers, and are moving to the peninsula in an ever rising tide. To me, it is the ideal place to write fiction.

Ideas for stories abound. Sailing on the Bay, watching otters at play in the creeks, talking with old watermen, exploring roads with names like Devil's Bottom, studying the history behind the memorials to Civil War dead; these were the kinds of events that led to the writing of the stories that follow. The tales cover the period from the 1840s to the 1990s. The characters in the stories as well as the oft-mentioned Bayberry Creek, are fictitious. But with a few exceptions, the towns, villages, rivers and creeks exist and references to Civil War battles, place names and events are accurate.

A Well-Kept Secret

A Well-Kept Secret

J ake and Jessie Bonneau learned by accident of the murder that had taken place in Aldersly Manor, the house that they wanted to buy. In the spring of 1917, the previous owner, a spinster named Jane Adams, had recently died. In accordance with her will, Aldersly Manor had immediately been put up for sale to pay the expenses of her funeral. Jake knew that the asking price was reasonable, but he had decided to make sure that the deceased had clear title to the manor before making an offer.

Jake and Jessie had recently moved to Lancaster County, on Virginia's Northern Neck—the peninsula that lies between the Rappahannock and Potomac Rivers. Jake was a reporter and he had accepted a position on a local newspaper. Because of his profession, he knew how to do legal research. He went to Lancaster Courthouse and did a thorough search of title records and court proceedings.

Among the musty court records, Jake found a copy of the title of the property and the will of Geoffrey Aldersly, the original builder of Aldersly Manor and the uncle of Jane Adams. The documents indicated that Geoffrey had left Aldersly manor to his niece and to his only son, Jane Adams and Reginald Aldersly. However, the terms of the will stated that Reginald was to receive his share of the estate only if the court found that he was innocent of the murder of James Berry, a local farmer, or that the murder was justifiable homicide. Jake learned from his neighbors that Reginald allegedly had run Berry through with a sword in the living room of the manor in the summer of 1860—fifteen years before Geoffrey's death in 1875. Jake did an exhaustive file search but could not find any evidence that Reginald was ever tried for the killing of James Berry. Fearing that he might not be able to obtain clear title to Aldersly Manor, Jake arranged a meeting with Michael Craver, the attorney handling the estate of Jane Adams.

At the meeting with Mr. Craver, Jake and Jessie were told that no one had seen or heard from Reginald Aldersly since the day of the killing, fifty-seven years before. He said that as attorney and executor for the deceased Miss Adams he could legally sell her estate.

"Jake," he said, "you don't have a thing to worry about if you purchase her house. Trust me." Jake was not totally convinced, but Jessie loved the house, so they signed the purchase agreement.

Jake and Jessie arrived to take possession of their new home early in the morning on the fourth of May 1917. The first thing they did was to make another, more leisurely, inspection of the exterior of the house and grounds. Aldersly Manor had been constructed on a ten-acre plot of land about a hundred feet back from the bank of Bayberry Creek, which emptied directly into the Chesapeake Bay. The house was almost boxlike, except that the entrance was centrally located with two large Georgian windows on either side. The severe look was further softened by four equally-spaced roof-dormers set between two large chimneys. The chimneys were massively built and gave the appearance of buttressing the ends of the house. At some time in the distant past, black walnut trees had been planted about sixty feet from each corner of the house. The trees stood over 120 feet high and Jake knew that the shade from their spreading limbs would help cool the house during the hot Virginia summers.

South of the house the property was cut by a small valley that ran down to the creek. As they walked up the long sloping hill which was one side of the valley, Jessie's eye was drawn to an expanse of blue, pink and white flowers just below the crest. When they reached the spot they found that the flowers were in two separate gardens connected by a flower-bordered path. They had just recently come into bloom. *That must be why I didn't notice them on our earlier visits*, thought Jessie. One garden surrounded a family burial plot, the other was a simple rectangular bed of hyacinths.

4

The neat and well-maintained burial plot contained three gravestones. The one on the left read: *GEOFFERY ALDERSLY, BORN 1803–DIED 1875*. The stone in the middle was manufactured from softer material and the engraving on it was weathered too badly to be read. The third gravestone was new and was placed to the right of the middle marker.

It read:

JANE ADAMS Born 1840– Died 1917.

I LOVE THEE WITH THE BREATH, SMILES,
TEARS, OF ALL MY LIFE! AND, IF GOD
CHOOSE, I SHALL BUT LOVE THEE BETTER
AFTER DEATH

Jessie Bonneau turned to her husband and pointed at the badly weathered grave stone.

"Jake, I wonder who is buried there and if there is a reason why Jane is buried next to that grave rather than next to her uncle?" Jake shook his head.

"I don't know, the records indicate that Geoffrey Aldersly's wife Julia, died shortly after giving birth to Reginald in England in 1835. That was at least a year before Geoffrey emigrated to Virginia, so we know the grave doesn't contain her remains. Jessie switched her attention to Jane's grave and said, "The quote from the Elizabeth Barrett Browning poem—who could Jane have been thinking of when she asked for it to be inscribed on her grave stone?" At this point Jake told his wife all he had learned about Jane Adams.

According to her obituary, which he looked up in his newspaper's files, she had been born in Yorkshire, England, in 1840. Her mother died when she was three years old and her father, Robert Adams, had told her that if anything ever happened to him, she was to go to Virginia to live with her uncle, her mother's brother. Robert Adams, a ship's captain, was lost at sea in 1856. Jane had loved her father very deeply and in obedience to his wish, she had moved to Aldersly Manor in 1857.

Jake said that he had talked to their minister after a Sunday service and he said that he had known Jane well. He said that she was a God-fearing woman and that she was intelligent, well-read and greatly loved by the young women of the church. For as long as he had known her—

5

nearly forty years—she had read the classics to these young women every Thursday evening in the living room of Aldersly Manor. He said that she was immensely fond of her uncle, for she spoke of him in loving terms for many years after his death.

Jake told Jessie that, while working on a newspaper article, he also had found an old story that described Jane as a Civil War heroine. The story told how, in 1864, she convinced the commandant of the Union prison at Point Lookout Maryland to allow her to treat the wounded and sick Rebels interned there. Point Lookout Prison was at the mouth of the Potomac River opposite the Northern Neck. Jane made the ten-mile crossing of the river in all kinds of weather to nurse the prisoners. The work was very dangerous since she also volunteered to be a secret courier for General Robert E. Lee. She carried messages to the Rebel prisoners about Lee's plan to free them in a surprise land and sea attack. The plan was found out and the Yankees learned from an informer that Jane was involved in the plot. She escaped by making a nighttime crossing of the Potomac during a storm. Her boat capsized near the Virginia shore. As friends dragged her to safety, she was heard to sob: "I'm found out. I'm found out! I can't go back! Who will nurse those poor boys now?"

After completing this brief description of Jane Adams's life, Jake suggested they go down the hill to their new home and begin making it livable. When they entered the house the shutters were closed and the interior lay in darkness. Jake felt his way to the four large Georgian windows. He opened the windows wide and unlatched and opened the shutters of each. Fresh air flooded into the house and the mid-morning sunshine patterned the floor with shadows from the frames of the small window panes. They began to explore the house and its furnishings in detail.

They had examined the interior of the house before purchasing it, but had not realized at the time that all the old furnishings conveyed with it. The ground floor consisted of a dining room, living room, office and pantry. As was common in nineteenth century homes, the kitchen was located in a separate building about thirty feet from a door which led from the pantry. The second floor held one large and three smaller bedrooms.

There was a considerable amount of needlepoint in the house. The chair seats were covered with it as well as the pillows on the old sofa. While much of it required cleaning, the quality of the work was excellent and Jessie intended to keep it. All of the drapes and curtains would have to be replaced, but here again Jessie marveled at the repair work that had been done on the material to keep it serviceable. Jessie thought. *Jane Adams may have spent a lot of time reading, but she certainly was a hardworking seamstress.*

"Jessie! Come and look at this." Jake was cleaning the dust from an oil painting that hung over the mantel of the great fireplace at one end of the living room. "I didn't even know it was hanging there until I started to check the condition of the oil lamps on the mantle." Jessie knew immediately what he meant. The painting was hung high enough above the mantel so that the light falling through the windows left it in deep shadow. It was meant to be illuminated by oil lamps which stood at either end of the mantle.

The painting portrayed two men in militia uniforms standing with an erect military bearing and a young woman sitting in front of them holding a small wicker sewing basket. One of the men appeared to be about sixty years old and the other in his mid-twenties. Both men in the picture had the same wide-set light blue eyes. The older man had a greying beard. The younger was clean shaven about the chin, but had a very dark mustache. He was tall, slim and broad-shouldered. One of his hands rested on his chest and held a locket between his thumb and forefinger. The girl in the oil painting was not beautiful but petite and pretty. She had long blonde curls which fell softly over her right shoulder. Her most striking feature was her eyes which were a lovely shade of green. The artist had caught something of her personality in her expression. She appeared happy, as if she were about to laugh. Jessie noticed all of this. Jake only said, "Look at the sewing basket the girl is holding. She must be Jane Adams! It's a family portrait."

Jessie said, "I think you're right. The resemblance of the two men is striking. The young man is really handsome. He's got to be Reginald Aldersly. He looks a bit arrogant, but not at all like a murderer to me." They examined the portrait carefully. It was done in fine detail. Individual hairs were visible in Geoffrey's beard. The wax gleamed on Reginald's mustache. Even the pattern of the needlepoint in the girl's sewing basket was clearly visible, as well as a shiny reflection off the blade of the scissors and the decorative handle of a small knife that could be seen sticking out of the basket. Out of curiosity Jake asked Jessie what the small knife was used for. She explained that a very sharp small knife was sometimes used to open seams. Then she sighed. "The painting is a beautiful piece of work. We'll clean it and leave it right where it is. Now let's get to work."

Just making the old manor house livable took nearly two weeks. Jessie selected the largest of the bedrooms for their own use. Two dormers looked down on Bayberry Creek and caught the early morning light. She was glad that it had not been Jane Adams's room. She knew that she would have been uncomfortable sleeping in the room where Jane had died.

When Jake and Jessie moved into the house, Jane's bedroom still contained her clothes and a few of her personal effects. None of these had any real value, but one day Jessie found a small wicker sewing basket while rummaging in a closet in the room. She recognized it as the one Jane was holding in the family portrait. She knew it must be very old, but it was still serviceable and quite attractive. She decided to keep it. As she examined its contents— needles, threads, thimbles, bits of cloth—she discovered a locket which contained a tightly curled lock of woman's hair. The hair was blonde. There was a simple inscription on the back. *Love is Eternal—JA.*

Without checking, she knew that the locket was the one Reginald Aldersly was wearing in the portrait. Showing the locket to Jake, she said, "I think that it's obvious that Reginald and Jane Adams were in love. See the blonde hair and the initials on the back of the locket — *JA* —."

Some days later, Jake was completing the refinishing of the bookcases that were built into the wall on either side of the fireplace in the study. The study was the name that Jessie had given the room. In reality it had more the look of an office than a study of the type one finds in a home. Aldersly Manor was originally part of a large working farm and Jake concluded that Geoffrey Aldersly probably had conducted much of the farm's business in the room. Scraping the accumulated paint of years from the oak bookcases was hard work. Unlike the other cases, the base of the one he was working on rested on top of a desk which had been fitted into a corner of the room. As he pushed the scraping tool into the back corner of the shelf, he heard something snap. Inspecting what he thought was a damaged wall panel, he discovered a small door. Only a latch had given way and he could see that there was something inside.

Jake reached in and quickly removed some rolled up needlework, a piece of paper, and an old book with the title "Journal" hand-printed in ink on its cover. Disappointed, Jake called Jessie and together they did a cursory examination of the material. An untitled poem had been hand-written on the piece of paper. Jessie read the poem aloud:

*He who loved me in silence was
here not long enough to know
how very deeply I loved him too.*

*Tho I still weep for the life we
never shared, I take solace that he
knows my love for him was true!*

*Who lusted after me and none did
tell, broke my heart and for
that will forever repent in hell.*

*Who took his love from me rests
in the dell. Know all, t'was I
who cared for him in sickness &
in well.*

Jane Adams

The "Journal" was a day to day record kept by Geoffrey Aldersly. As Jake flipped randomly through the book, he saw that it was a record of events and anything that was of personal interest to Geoffrey. The "Journal" included remarks on family matters, social events, and farm operations; what he paid for cotton seed in 1835, the condition of his corn crop on 1 July 1836, the name of one man who was a good worker and another who was not. The third object, the needlework, was not at all exceptional. It contain a couple of lines of poetry and the name of the poet, "O. Khayyam." The material was covered with dust and appeared to be very fragile. They set it aside.

Jake thought the journal might shed some light on the events surrounding James Berry's death. Placing his scraper in his toolbox, he opened the book again and began to go through it carefully, a page at a time. It was hard going. The paper had deteriorated with age and the yellowed pages tended to crack and crumble as he turned them. The writing was small and the book covered many years. The sun was setting and the room was beginning to darken when he found the first reference to James Berry.

It was a simple acknowledgment that the man was a good neighbor and hard worker. James had apparently worked for Geoffrey during the corn harvest. The year of the entry was 1858. Jake found two more references to Mr. Berry. The second reference recorded that James Berry and Reginald had located the site of the "old dry well" and were going to use it to store a freshly made barrel of blackberry brandy which they wished to age. According to the journal, they had dumped dry sand into the well, creating a floor, twenty feet below ground level. The temperature there was fifty-five degrees. Ideal, they thought, for aging the brandy. The date was July 1, 1860.

In the third reference, dated only five days later, Geoffrey wrote out the testimony he had given to the sheriff concerning the killing of James Berry. According to the text, Geoffrey had been returning home on horseback from Kilmarnock, a nearby village, when he heard angry shouting coming from the manor. At first the voices were indistinguishable. As he dismounted and rushed to the manor door, he heard Reginald yell, "Take your hands off of her, you lout." Geoffrey then heard Jane scream.

According to the journal, Geoffrey rushed into the house, where he found Jane lying on the couch and weeping in near hysteria. Reginald stood nearby with a bloody sword in his hand. James Berry's body lay sprawled on the floor in a slowly spreading pool of blood. When Geoffrey asked what had happened, his son replied, "He got what he deserved for putting his hands on her." At this point Geoffrey's distraught niece ran from the room. The following exchange then took place. "Son, he was unarmed. They may hang you for this!"

"That is not likely Father, for they will have to find me first and there are many places where a man can hide in the West." After this exchange Reginald went into the office, took a bag of gold coins from a recent cotton sale and left the house. He was never seen again. Geoffrey wrote that his last words to his son were, "The authorities will overtake you within a day."

According to the journal, the sheriff arrived late on the day of the killing. That evening and the following morning he checked at all the steamship landings along the rivers and the nearby Chesapeake Bay. No one recalled having seen Reginald. Riders were sent on fast horses to the western counties; Richmond, Westmoreland, and King George. But no trace was ever found of the murderer.

If Geoffrey was deeply concerned about his son's disappearance, he made no mention of it in the journal. But in the days immediately following the murder, his love and concern for his niece were made obvious by his frequent references to her emotional state. Then, from the spring of 1861 until the last entry in the book in 1865, the remarks focused on the inevitability of civil war between the states and then on the actual events of the war itself. It was well beyond dinner time and it was already very dark by the time Jake finished reading the journal. He resolved to review everything with Jessie in the morning.

The following morning Jake showed Jessie the entries in the journal. After she read them all, she turned to Jake. "Well now we know what happened, but I'm still not sure why. It looks to me like Reginald caught James pawing Jane or worse and in a fit of rage ran him through with his sword. But if he loved her that much, why didn't he come back for her? There is nothing to indicate that they ever heard from him again!"

Jessie was rapidly losing interest in the Reginald and Jane affair, as she called it. Her interest had shifted to cleaning and restoring the needlepoint that the previous occupant of the house had left her. A few days later she decided to take another look at the piece Jake had found in Geoffrey Aldersly's desk in the study. It had been rolled and the outside layer was covered with dust. It was the only piece of needlework in the house that looked like it had been given absolutely no care. She unrolled the piece carefully and read the lines of poetry aloud to Jake:

And not a drop that from our cup we throw
For hyacinths to drink of, but may steal below
To quench the fire of anguish in some eye
There hidden—far beneath, and long ago.

O. Khayyam

Jessie looked at Jake. "I think she must have sewn this shortly after James Berry's murder. It's morbid. Who is this O. Khayyam anyway?"

Jake chuckled. "He was a Persian and he wrote poetry, very sensual stuff. A translation of his work was printed under the title, the Rubaiyat of Omar Khayyam. I remember reading some of it when I attended William and Mary. I'm taking the steamboat *Lancaster* to Annapolis next week. I have to interview some politicians. I'll buy a copy of the Rubaiyat for you while I'm there." Jake was as good as his word and purchased the Rubaiyat in Annapolis. The steamer trip back to Kilmarnock took the better part of the night. Once aboard the *Lancaster* he decided to read the copy of the Rubaiyat before retiring.

11

Eventually he came to the passage that was on the needlepoint. *And not a drop that from our cup we throw—For earth to drink of, but may steal below—To quench the fire of anguish in some eye there hidden— far beneath, and long ago.*

Jake continued reading, the book contained just over one hundred quatrains, and he finished it in short order. As he placed it in his briefcase, he had the uneasy feeling that something was wrong. He wondered what it might be, but then decided to take a nap and let his subconscious work on it. This little mental trick usually worked well for him. And it did this time. Only it took a little longer than usual.

Two days later Jake and Jessie had just fallen asleep in their big brass bed when Jake woke with a start. His subconscious had solved the problem of the poem. *Jane had changed a word in the quatrain when she recorded it in needlepoint.* Jake's newsman's intuition told him that he was on to something. As he slowly fell back to sleep he resolved that, in the morning, he would look again at the contents of the hiding place in the study.

The next morning, as the sun edged up over the loblolly pines on the far side of Bayberry Creek and sent soft yellow shafts of light through the dormer windows of the bedroom, Jake finished dressing. He went directly to the desk in the study. He picked up the contents of the hiding place and took the three objects to a table next to one of the large Georgian windows where the light was better.

He set aside the needlepoint and journal and looked at the words on the single sheet of yellowed paper.

He who loved me in silence was
here not long enough to know
how very deeply I loved him too.

Tho I still weep for the life we
never shared, I take solace that
he knows my love for him was true!

Who lusted after me and none did
tell, broke my heart and for
that will forever repent in hell

Who took his love from me rests
in the dell. Know all, t'was I
who cared for him in sickness &
in well.

J. Adams

Jake studied the verses. Who were they written for? For that matter who were they written about? He and Jessie had assumed that James Berry had attacked Jane and that Reginald had come to her aid and in a rage killed Berry. The evidence was only circumstantial. Maybe they were wrong. What did the last two verses mean?

In frustration Jake opened the journal and started through it again. This time he wrote down the substance of each entry that mentioned Reginald, Jane or James. James was mentioned only three times: Geoffrey noted that he was an excellent workman. He mentioned the placing of the brandy in the dry well. And he recounted what he knew of James' murder. There were surprisingly few entries about Reginald in the book. They included: A reference to his commission in the militia. A negative comment that he "inclined to the grape" too much. And a handful of complimentary remarks about his successful marketing of the farm's products. On the other hand there were numerous references to Jane. It was obvious from the text that Geoffrey regarded his niece very highly. The first reference to her must have been shortly after her arrival. It simply said she had arrived from England, that she was lovely and reminded him of his wife, Julia. Thereafter he remarked on each glowing report the minister had passed to him about her; about the quality of her sewing and housekeeping; and frequently about her caring for the sick of the household.

Jake began to review everything he knew about Jane. Her sewing; her love of poetry and the classics; the poem from the hiding place; the poetry on the needlepoint, the flower gardens that she must have planted, her bravery, her obvious skill as a nurse. He hesitated. Her skill as a nurse... Her poem mentioned caring for someone in sickness and in .... According to the journal, that person would most likely have been Geoffrey or Reginald not James. Or maybe the poem was about both James and Reginald. Suddenly Jake thought about the verse from the Rubyiat of Omar Khayyam and he thought he knew why Reginald Aldersly had not returned for Jane.

A feeling of dread came over him as he began to piece together a

13

solution to Reginald's disappearance. But, he said aloud, "It's like prospecting for gold, despite what the surface evidence indicates, you never know if it's really down there unless you dig." By this time it was late afternoon, but he went looking for tools anyway.

After gathering up a pitchfork, shovel, and an armful of garden stakes, Jake walked to the hyacinth garden at the head of the small valley near the house. The flower garden measured only about fifteen by twenty feet. He started at one corner and drove the tangs of the pitchfork into the ground. The tangs were about fourteen inches long and it took considerable effort to drive them into the earth. Once they were in all the way he pulled them out, moved about twelve inches in a diagonal direction and repeated the process, trying all the while to damage as few hyacinths as possible. After ten minutes his fork hit something solid about twelve inches below the surface. He pulled it out and pushed a stake into one of the tang holes. He kept doing this until he had defined the shape of the object beneath the ground.

When Jake saw the circular pattern of the stakes, he knew that he had found what he had been looking for. He went back to the manor, found a lantern and returned. Then he began to dig in earnest. Within fifteen minutes he had excavated the area inside the stakes down to the object below. It was a well covering, about forty-eight inches across. The wood had been covered with a thick layer of tar and copper sheeting. *Probably from an old ship's bottom*, he thought. With a fallen tree limb as a lever, he pried off the well cover. The cover had three holes drilled in it, equidistant around the edge and about twelve inches from the center. Two were the same diameter and the third was considerably larger. This third hole contained the remains of a plug, obviously driven in downward from the top of the cover.

A moldy stench emanated from the well. The walls, which appeared to be brick, were covered with mildew and a sort of slime. Jake dropped a clod of dirt into the black hole. It struck the bottom with a dull thud. *It's dry*, thought Jake.

It was difficult to see down in the well, not only because of its depth, but also because it was dusk and darkness was rapidly approaching. He lit the lantern, tied on a cord, and began lowering it into the well. When the lantern was about six feet below the surface he stopped. He could see what appeared to be two footholds cut into the brick. The day had been warm but the sweat running down his back and neck felt cold. A wave of nausea caused sour stomach fluid to rise in his throat. He shivered. He knew what he was going to find.

As the oil lantern was lowered its yellow light only dimly lit the floor of the dry well. But it was enough. Jake saw the remains of a crude rope ladder, a cask, fragments of a skeleton, some gold coins, and the badly tarnished handle of a small, decorative, seamstress' knife. *My God*, thought Jake. *Reginald was going to hide in the dry well until the sheriff gave up the search, then head out West. With his feet in the footholds he could move the well cover back in place, then climb down the rope ladder. But Jane must have seen him enter the well. She cut his rope ladder, probably where it was looped through the two holes in the well cover. She pushed a plug into his air hole and left him to suffocate or worse; die of starvation. She must have watered the HYACINTHS over his head, caring for his grave, all the remaining years of her life.*

Jake returned the well cover to its place, covered it with dirt, replanted the hyacinths, and went to see attorney Craver.

In the weeks that followed Jessie made the old manor into a home. All the interior walls were painted white to brighten the rooms. The needlework was cleaned and restored to its former beauty and the oak bookcases were sanded smooth and stained a rich golden hue. She kept the Aldersly family portrait hanging in its place above the great fireplace. The golden locket that hung about Reginald's neck in the painting actually seemed to shine at times in the flickering light of the oil lamps.

One evening, while looking at the painting, she said to Jake, "Reginald sure was handsome, I can see how Jane could have fallen in love with him."

To which Jake responded, "It was James she loved, not Reginald. He was the one love of her life and she loved him passionately and completely. It is most likely James that is buried next to her in the old family plot." Jessie's eyebrows went up, "If that's so, why did she give Reginald the locket? It said *LOVE IS ETERNAL—JA*." Jake said. "She didn't, his mother Julia Aldersly left it for him!" Jane was still doubtful. "But how can you be so SURE she loved James!"

"Trust me," Jake said, "I know!"

EPILOGUE

Jake had paid a visit to attorney Craver immediately after finding the old well and its contents. To his surprise the attorney simply sighed when Jake told him what he had found. With a sad expression he said,

"You're a good investigative reporter Jake. Yes, Jane Adams murdered her cousin Reginald. She loved James Berry with her whole being and the advances of Reginald, who was after all her first cousin, offended her deeply. In the presence of both men, she firmly rejected the one and pledged her love to the other. But to her horror, in a jealous rage, Reginald Aldersly killed James Berry, the one she loved with the very *breath of all of her life*. In a visceral rage she took her revenge."

"But how do you know all this?" Jake asked. Craver continued. "Jane did not want to die without confessing her guilt. She knew that there would be a question about whether there was a clear title to Aldersly Manor and that someone would investigate. That's why she left the clues in the desk. But as the end of her life neared she worried that whoever bought her house might not recognize the clues she had left behind. In a letter enclosed with the will she mailed to me a few days before her death, she confessed to Reginald's murder."

Craver looked directly at Jake. "I suppose that while her uncle Geoffrey was alive she felt that if he learned what she had done, it would kill him. I don't know why she kept silent after he died, but I think that she spent the last fifty-seven years of her life burdened with her guilt and trying to make up for her crime. I have destroyed her confession. I intend never to speak of it to anyone again. You have clear title to your home, you know better than most the kind of woman she was."

Jake looked at the old attorney, nodded and without saying a word left the office.

Outrageous

Outrageous

Ed and Sarah were sitting under a magnificent old beech tree on a hill overlooking the sparkling green waters of Bayberry Creek. The day was warm, it was spring, and the curved limbs of the huge beech lifted thousands of newly opened leaves to the noonday sun. The sky was a flawless blue and the sun combined with a light breeze to make a shimmering, translucent canopy of the bright green leaves. Sarah loved the quiet splendor of the place. Several weeks earlier, in this very spot, she had accepted Ed's marriage proposal.

Ed Pelter had the look of a man who spent his days outdoors. And indeed, as a boat builder he worked long hours each day in the fresh air and sunshine of a small boatyard on the creek. Over the years the constant hauling and lifting of boat timber had kept him fit and added muscle to his stocky frame. At twenty-six, there were already hints of grey in his short, sandy blonde hair. His eyes were a rich brown and his facial expression seemed to imply great friendliness. Normally he laughed and smiled easily and often. On this beautiful day, however, Ed was an unhappy man. As Ed and Sarah talked, he held her hand in his.

"Sarah, I don't understand your father. This is 1923, not the Middle Ages. Does he really think he can stop you from marrying me? I'm not the world's best catch, but I can provide for you and make you happy." Sarah squeezed Ed's hand. "Ed you are the world's best catch, but it's not my happiness that concerns my father." Ed thought about yesterday's meeting with Sarah's father, Frank Brown. He had gone to their farm to ask for Sarah's hand.

Sarah had taken him into the parlor where her father was sitting in an old oak rocker, drawing softly on an unlit pipe. He was wearing a freshly pressed work shirt and a clean pair of faded blue denim coveralls. Ed noticed that although his face was stern, there were laugh lines around his eyes. He remembered thinking, *he looks stern now, but there was a time when he was a happy man. Maybe he's just tired from all the farm work.* Ed knew that Mr. Brown owned and worked over five hundred acres of prime farmland with his son, John, and employed two hired hands.

Ed had met Frank Brown several times before, and although he had not said much, he had never been unfriendly. So when Sarah told her father that Ed had something very important to discuss with him and he did not respond, Ed nervously launched into the speech that he had prepared. "Mr. Brown, Sarah and I are very much in love. I have asked her to marry me and she has accepted. I've come to ask your blessing on the marriage." Before Ed could go on, Frank Brown rose quickly to his feet and stood, facing him squarely. Taking his pipe from his mouth, he looked at Sarah momentarily and then fixed his deep blue eyes directly on Ed's. "I'm not getting any younger and this farm is too big for just my son John and me. Would you be willing to settle here with Sarah and share the burden? Mind you, Sarah and John will inherit the place someday."

Ed swallowed hard. It was not what he had expected to hear. He said, "Mr. Brown, your offer is very generous, but I can't accept. I'm a boat builder, I would not be happy as a farmer. But I can support Sarah. Business at the boatyard where I work is good, and my job there is secure. I have several hundred dollars in a savings account." He was about to say that, apart from his job, he was building a boat and when it was finished, he was going to sell it and use the money and his savings as a down payment on a house.

With a wave of his hand Frank Brown cut him off. It seemed to Ed that at that moment Frank Brown's eyes turned from blue to an icy grey. "No! You cannot marry my daughter. I will not allow it. The very idea is outrageous! It's outrageous! Outrageous!" Each repetition of the word was louder and more forceful. "I offer you part of the best

20

farm on the Northern Neck and you want to build boats! My daughter will not marry a no-account boatyard worker!"

Ed was taken back by the fury of the outburst. He felt Sarah tugging at his arm and he saw tears in her eyes. He put his arm around her and drew her to his side. Looking at the man who had caused her pain, he fought to control his anger. He was about to reply when he saw the pleading look in Sarah's eyes and allowed himself to be led from the room.

Sitting under the beech tree, remembering the meeting, Ed felt angry again. Sarah guessed what he was thinking. She moved closer and took both his hands in hers. "Ed, it's not you. My father doesn't want me to leave. I've looked after him and John since my mother died four years ago. It's not just that I cook and do the washing and clean after them. I bear a strong resemblance to my mother and remind him of her. And then there's the farm. He and my mother loved it. He's not a young man anymore and he doesn't think that John will be able to handle it alone after he's gone."

She could see that he was still very upset. She tried to change the subject for awhile. "How is the work coming on your boat?"

Ed almost smiled. "I'll finish it in the next couple of weeks. I'm making sure it's the best boat I've ever built. When the time comes, I want it to sell." Ed should have guessed what the next question would be, but he didn't. "Are you going to name it after me? Lots of husbands name their boats after their mothers or wives." Ed was momentarily confused. "But we aren't married..." Before he could say more she kissed him softly on the lips and said, "So let's go see Reverend Wright and fix that."

Reverend Wright understood their situation immediately. Sarah and her brother attended services regularly, but Frank Brown had not set foot in the minister's church since his wife had died. It was common knowledge that he had not resigned himself to his wife's death and that he was a withdrawn and bitter man. The minister told Sarah that he was concerned about Frank's reaction once he found out about her marriage to Ed.

Sarah looked at the minister and her future husband. "Despite what you may think, my father loves me. It's just that he can't accept that I must leave him. But I think that my leaving will help him get on with his life. We'll have a quiet wedding, and I'll write him a short note that my brother, John, will give him after the ceremony. But I'm afraid that if he finds out we are getting married, he'll try to find me and take me home, married or not. If we can get away for a few weeks, I think he will come to his senses."

Ed looked at her and grinned, "Leave the getaway to me." Ed and Sarah decided to get married in two weeks, on Saturday, May 6th. Not coincidentally, it was also the date of the Kilmarnock Festival.

Reverend Wright wrote the date on his calendar and smiled at them. "And who will be the witnesses?" Sarah spoke up immediately. "Jean Smith will be my bridesmaid. Ed, you have no family and you like Jean's husband Charlie; couldn't he be your best man?" In point of fact it was through Charlie that Ed had met Sarah, and she knew they were more than just casual acquaintants. So it was no surprise to Sarah when he said, "Yes, of course, I'll ask him."

Sarah and Jean lived on neighboring farms and had grown up together. They were best friends and confidantes. Both were nineteen years old, medium height, slim with light brown hair and hazel eyes. Their resemblance was close enough that people often mistook them for sisters. Sarah had been the bridesmaid when Jean and Charlie were married only a year ago. It had occurred to Sarah that she could borrow Jean's wedding dress and that Jean could wear the orchid-colored dress that she had worn as her bridesmaid.

While Sarah was thinking about the wedding, Ed was pondering how he would spirit Sarah away from the Northern Neck. In 1923, there were several bustling small towns within eight to nine miles of Frank Brown's farm at the Bay end of Virginia's Northern Neck —the land between the Potomac and Rappahannock rivers. Kilmarnock was the closest. The commerce of all of the towns centered on farming and the harvesting of fish, crabs and oysters from the Chesapeake Bay and its tributaries. Though prosperous, the towns were isolated and could be conveniently reached only by the steamboat lines that plied the Bay. Each town had its own steamboat dock. Kilmarnock's was on Indian Creek, which flowed directly into the Chesapeake. If Ed and Sarah were to leave the Northern Neck, the normal way would be by steamer. Frank Brown would know this.

In the following two weeks Sarah saw Ed only twice. He told her that he had made all the arrangements for their escape—as he put it— and their honeymoon. He had rented a small cottage on a beach near Deltaville on the Middle Neck, south of the Rappahannock River. The rent was modest and they could stay there as long as necessary.

Sarah looked forward to her wedding with great happiness, but it was a difficult period because she had to hide her happiness from her father. John was going to give her away, so of course he knew of the wedding plans. He managed to keep her father busy while Sarah packed her bags and carried them to Jean's for safekeeping.

On Saturday, May 6th, Sarah put on her orchid dress and told her father that she and John were going to the Kilmarnock Festival. He commented on how pretty she looked in the dress and that it seemed too nice to wear just to a festival. She had a moment of near panic when her father said to John that he ought not to be going to town when there was so much farmwork to be done. John got out of the predicament nicely by saying that he had to pick up some fence wire at the hardware anyway. Sarah felt uneasy about lying to her father, so on the way to the church they stopped at the festival, where she bought a small gift for Jean.

They met Reverend Wright at the church. He showed them to a small room off the foyer where Jean helped Sarah into her wedding dress. Once that was done, Jean slipped into Sarah's orchid dress and they were ready. The two left the small room, passed through the doors of the foyer and into the church where John was waiting. The entire front of the church was filled with white and pink dogwood, white azaleas, and roses of the deepest red that Sarah had ever seen. The flowers were the wedding gift of Charlie and Jean. As John escorted his sister slowly down the aisle to the wedding march, she saw Ed standing amid the flowers waiting for her. He smiled and her eyes glowed.

After the wedding, Sarah changed out of her wedding dress in the little room off the foyer. Then Charlie and Jean drove the newlyweds to the Kilmarnock steamboat landing. When they arrived, Charlie jumped out of the buggy and ran into the office. In a few moments he came back waving two tickets. "The bridal suite," he said triumphantly as he handed the tickets to Ed. A sign at the foot of the dock indicated that the steamer *Lancaster* left at 5:00 P.M. It was only 4:00 P.M. Sarah looked at Ed and said, "Ed, I hope the steamer leaves before father arrives. This is the first place he'll look after he finds out we're married."

When John returned home, his father was still out in the fields. Anxious to avoid a confrontation, he placed the note that Sarah had written for her father on the kitchen table and left the house. Shortly thereafter Frank Brown came in and found the piece of paper. As he read it, his usual stern appearance changed to a look of pain and disbelief. The note read: *Dearest dad, by the time you read this note, Ed and I will be married. I love him with all my heart. I love you too. Please try to understand. I will write you in a couple of weeks. Love, Sarah.*

Frank bounded up the stairs to Sarah's bedroom. He checked her dresser and closet. Most of her things were gone. With a moan he ran down the stairs and nearly smashed through the screen on the kitchen door. He ran to the barn and hitched up the horse and buggy. He mumbled to himself, "She always said that she wanted to be married in Wright's church."

When he arrived at the church, Reverend Wright tried to reason with him, but Frank would have none of it. He spat out, "Where did they go?" The minister shook his head. "They only said they were going away for a few weeks, they didn't say where."

There's only one way to leave the Neck, Frank thought. *The steamer.* He arrived at the Kilmarnock landing in time to see the aft end of the steamer *Lancaster* disappear around a bend in Indian Creek. He ran up to the ticket window. "Did you see a young couple board the steamer? Girl wearing an orchid dress, she's about five foot two, light brown hair, hazel eyes. She'd be with a young man, a little taller than me."

The woman behind the ticket counter, sensing the anger in Frank's voice, spoke softly. "Yes, I sold a young man tickets for the bridal suite. The young lady who boarded with him wore an orchid dress and I think she fit your description. But the steamer has just left. If it's an emergency, you might be able to catch them at one of the landings farther up the Bay."

Frank had a decision to make. There were a half dozen stops the steamer would make before it departed the Northern Neck for Baltimore. The problem was that the stops were only a short distance by water but a much longer distance by land. If he chased the steamer from port to port and arrived just a little late each time, he was going to wear his horse out. Frank decided to head directly for the *Lancaster's* last stop on the Neck—Tiper's Landing.

He was about half a mile from Tiper's Landing when Frank heard the *Lancaster's* whistle. He thought, *she's just pulling into the landing, I'm going to make it.* Before he heard the whistle he had begun to have second thoughts about what he was doing. But the sound of the whistle put all such thoughts from his mind. He would save his daughter from this outrageous mistake.

Drovers were still pushing some cattle aboard the cargo deck when he arrived at the landing. He went aboard and walked along the passenger deck looking at the crowds of people who were leaning over

24

the ship's railing talking to friends and family ashore. It seemed like he had hardly begun his search when he heard someone shout: "All ashore that's going ashore." *Damn*, he thought, *I'm not going to have enough time to find them before the boat leaves.* He rushed back to the gangplank in a panic and purchased a roundtrip ticket to Baltimore from the purser. As the lines were being cast off, Frank went to the stern of the steamer and resumed his search.

Proceeding toward the bow, he walked slowly through the public rooms; the smoker, the salon and the dining room. High-backed chairs concealed the identity of their occupants, and the many small groups of travelers slowed his search. When he was satisfied that they were not in the public rooms, he moved back outdoors. He saw them as he approached the forward observation deck. Her orchid dress stood out clearly in the late afternoon sunshine.

The steamer was leaving the mouth of the Great Wicomico River. They were standing arm in arm with their backs toward him. They were admiring the verdant shoreline of the Northern Neck and pointing at the homes along Sandy Point. The soft murmur of voices coming from a small group of travelers, the low throb of the steam engine as it turned the ship's large paddle wheel, and the lapping of the waves against the side of the steamer prevented the couple from hearing his footsteps as he rushed toward them.

"Sarah!" The girl jumped at the sound of the name and swung about, facing him. "Why, Mr. Brown, what a nice surprise. What are you doing here?"

Frank recognized Charlie and Jean at once and knew that he had been tricked. As he looked at them, Charlie put his arm around Jean and drew her to his side. It was the instinctive reaction of two people in love. Frank remembered that when he had refused Ed's request for Sarah's hand, Ed had done the same thing. He remembered the movement and the deep expression of hurt in Sarah's eyes that had caused Ed to draw her near. At that moment Frank realized that he had been a fool. *Ed loves Sarah as deeply as I loved her mother. Why didn't I see that when he asked for her hand? Now, what has become of them?*

Looking at Sarah's distraught father, Charlie reflected on what had happened that afternoon. After he had purchased the steamer tickets, he got back into the buggy and, much to Sarah's surprise they drove several hundred yards down the road along Indian Creek to some private boat slips.

Ed helped Sarah out of the buggy and with a wave of his hand said, "Mrs. Pelter—your yacht." It was Ed's new boat. Sarah went over and looked at the transom. She laughed. "Ed, you didn't name it after me after all. But it's still beautiful."

Ed turned to Jean. "Jean, it's customary for the groom to give his best man a gift." He handed the steamer tickets back to Charlie. "Charlie will explain everything to you."

Ed and Sarah boarded their boat. Ed started the engine and cast off the lines. Then, waving to the couple on the dock, the newlyweds left in a downpour of rice. As Ed and Sarah looked back, Charlie and Jean were in an animated conversation that ended in a bout of laughter as they walked toward the steamboat *Lancaster*.

Ed and Sarah spent their wedding night in a secluded cove, surrounded by flowering dogwood, the bright green leaves of trees in springtime, and wildflowers. They shared the cove only with several flocks of waterfowl , including some beautiful white muted swans which were on their journey north.

One week later, Frank was talking to one of his few friends, a crabber who worked out of Indian Creek. Frank had been thinking about Ed and Sarah, and he had a hunch that they may have left Kilmarnock by a small boat. He asked his friend if he had seen any new boats on the creek lately. The crabber replied, "I've only seen one boat that I didn't recognize in the last month. Saw it last Saturday. It was brand spankin' new. But I remember it because it had a funny name," Frank said. "And what was that?" The crabber said. "Outrageous." Frank frowned for a moment, then slowly a grin spread across his face.

EPILOGUE

Two weeks after the wedding Sarah wrote her father and gave him her address. Frank responded by mail immediately. Shortly thereafter Ed and Sarah visited Frank. He apologized for his behavior. Sarah even thought she heard a catch in his voice when he said the farm wasn't the same without her, although he quickly assured her that he and John were making out just fine. When her father, Ed, and John made plans to celebrate the fourth of July by taking her fishing, Sarah knew that they were a family once again.

In the years that followed the wedding, Frank's neighbors saw a slow but steady change in him. He started going to church services regularly again and was even seen at church socials with the woman who sold tickets at the Kilmarnock steamboat landing.

In 1925, Sarah presented Ed with the first of three children, a girl. In order to provide for his enlarging family, Ed quit the boatyard and started his own boatbuilding business on Bayberry Creek. The extraordinary care and attention to detail that he put into his first boat had paid off. Among those who saw it was a sportsman who persuaded Ed to build him a boat. Ed quickly demonstrated that he had a fine eye for the design of sport-fishing craft and soon had more business than he could handle. His boats were noted for quality and durability, but everyone said that his prices were ....!

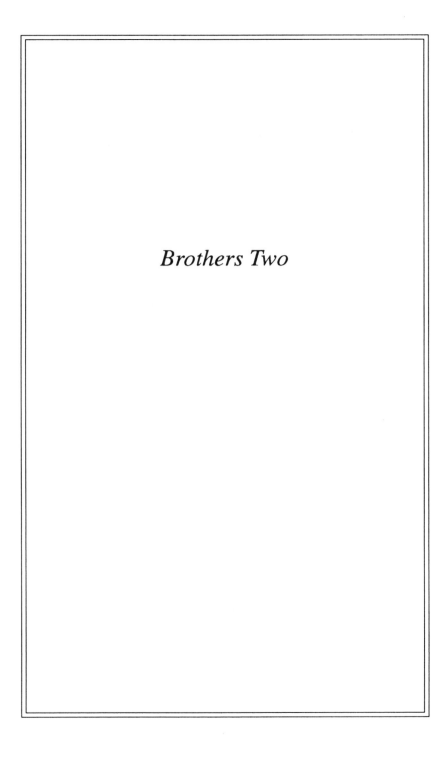

Brothers Two

Brothers Two

Joe Kinderly had been sitting at the end of his boat dock for over an hour, waiting for nightfall. While he sat there the gray evening sky darkened and the autumn colors of the trees along Bayberry Creek changed slowly from yellow and rust to gray and deep brown. The tide was going out and in the quiet evening air a faint smell of decaying vegetation, drifting up from the muck at the water's edge, added to his general discomfort. His stomach was usually upset before he made a run out on the Chesapeake to pick up drugs, but tonight he also had a nagging feeling that he had forgotten something.

A short distance behind Joe, the dock widened from six to about twenty feet. In the center of the wider portion a small building had been constructed and the dock formed a walkway around it. Joe's boat, the *Brothers Two*, was tied to the walkway, opposite the door of the building. In the rapidly fading evening light, a single light-bulb above the door barely illuminated a hand-lettered red and white sign that read, *Kinderly's Marine Engine Repair and Towing Service.*

After a hard day's work, sitting in the cool evening air had caused Joe's muscles to stiffen. But with a soft groan, he forced his slim, six-foot frame erect, pushed a shock of brown hair from his blue eyes, and walked slowly down the dock and entered the building. In a few minutes he emerged carrying a gray instrument case in one hand and a small outboard motor in the other. He set the motor on the dock, stepped down into his boat, and placed the gray case on the boat's instrument panel.

The *Brothers Two* was a twenty-six foot, wooden fishing boat. Similar boats could be found in dozens of the small creeks that empty into the Chesapeake Bay. It had a powerful inboard engine and a bracket on the transom for a smaller trolling motor. The boat's only distinguishing features were its name, painted on a board that was mounted on the transom, and a heavy-duty towing tripod. Joe unbolted the steel towing tripod from the boat's deck and, with the help of a gin pole, hoisted it onto the dock. After unscrewing the board on which the boat's name was painted, he tossed it up on the dock too. Then from where he stood in the boat, he reached out and lifted the outboard motor off the dock and lowered it onto its bracket on the boat's transom.

The motor was a quiet-running five HP model, manufactured in 1990 and only a year old. Joe covered the motor with a peculiar-looking spherical object that he had taken from under a cheap plastic life raft, which lay partially inflated on the boat's deck. He placed the outboard's gear shift in neutral and with a sharp pull on the lanyard, started the motor. The spherical object was a silencer and, with it in place, anyone more than a hundred feet away couldn't hear the motor running.

After setting the outboard's speed control to idle, he returned to the boat's instrument panel and opened the gray box which contained a portable Global Positioning System, a small navigational device that acquired position data from orbiting satellites. These devices were becoming commonplace on small boats that ventured offshore, and Joe had bought this one second-hand. With a few key strokes the GPS could provide compass bearings that would allow him to travel from point to point in total darkness or fog. He turned the GPS on and fastened it to the instrument panel.

Joe untied his dock lines, eased the softly purring boat out into Bayberry Creek and headed for the Chesapeake. He motored along without running lights, staying in the center of the creek by carefully monitoring his depth sounder and compass. This would be the fourth time that he had made a nighttime drug run. After tonight, he intended never to do it again.

As he entered Chesapeake Bay he was sure his neighbors along the creek had neither seen nor heard him. Offshore, to the south, he could see the intermittent flash of the Windmill Point Light, marking the entrance to the Rappahannock River. Out of habit he counted off four seconds and, as expected, saw the flash of the light pierce the darkness again. At a much greater distance, both north and south, red and green navigation markers faintly blinked on and off.

Joe was no stranger to this nighttime aspect of the Bay. When he was still in high school he and his brother Tom had often left home before dawn to empty their crab pots at first light so that he could be on time for classes. Their father had been a waterman and had taught them well. He died when Joe was ten and Tom was eighteen. Joe never knew his mother, she had died when he was just an infant. After his father's death, Tom was father and brother to Joe.

Joe joined the National Guard right after high school. The military testing program identified his aptitude for electronics and he was trained as a radar operator. His Guard unit had been sent to the Gulf War, and he had trouble finding a job when he came home. Finally, his brother, Tom, had talked a friend into giving him part-time work at a local marina. The mechanic there taught him all he knew about engine repair.

Tom was the only person in the world that Joe really cared about, until he met Amy.

The summer after his return from the war, Joe's friends from his National Guard unit formed a softball team to play in a local "Volunteer Firemen's Festival" tournament. Playing third base in one of the games, Joe chased a pop fly into the watching crowd. Looking up, trying to keep the ball in sight, he tripped over a bat bag and went headlong into the dirt. As he rose to his feet he heard a soft, laughing voice say, "Way to keep your eye on the ball." As he turned to jog back onto the playing field, a pretty girl in a nicely filled out pair of shorts and softball shirt took off her ball cap and beat some dirt off his shoulder. That was their introduction.

Within a few weeks the young couple were seen together everywhere and in less than a year the deepening affection between Joe and Amy grew into love. Amy's parents watched this development with some apprehension. Amy was their only child and they were concerned about her future with Joe. He had only a part-time job. There was no family farm, no family business, and in fact his future prospects looked dim. But Joe and Amy were deeply in love, and they began to talk about marriage. Joe was acutely aware that Amy's family was worried about their daughter's future with him.

As he left the creek that night Joe was thinking that after he was paid for tonight's business, Amy's family wouldn't have to be concerned anymore.

After motoring straight out into the Bay for about three miles, Joe turned off the outboard and started the more powerful inboard engine. He checked the GPS for the compass bearing to the location near the middle of the Bay where he had agreed to meet the drug runners. He estimated that he would make the rendezvous in thirty minutes. He arrived early and as he waited in the darkness he thought about how he had gotten into drug running.

As he always did when he had a problem, Joe had turned to his brother for advice about how to provide for his and Amy's future. One evening, after dinner in the small apartment they shared, Joe told Tom how deeply he loved Amy. With a sigh, he shook his head sadly, "Tom, I don't have anything. Before we can get married I've got to find a way to make more money." Listening to the emotion in his brother's voice, Tom was deeply moved by Joe's unhappiness.

At thirty, Tom had already worked on the water for nearly thirteen years. He tended crab traps from spring until fall and during the cold-weather months he worked the oyster beds. Tom never pretended to have a head for business, but raising a younger brother alone had taught him the value of money. As often as he could, he put what little extra cash he had into a savings account. Now he decided to use his life's savings to help Joe.

After some discussion, Joe said that he thought he could make a success of a marine engine repair and towing business. With Tom's money, they bought Joe an old wooden boat and repaired it. Tom worked evenings on the boat's hull and Joe rebuilt the engine. Once the boat was repaired, Tom loaned Joe enough money to lease a building on Bayberry Creek, within walking distance of their apartment. Together they repaired and equipped the building as best as they could with the last of Tom's savings.

Joe opened for business in the fall of 1991. He never expected that it would be easy, but within three months he knew that he was in serious financial trouble. Because of the economic recession, most fishermen and nearly all oystermen were doing their own engine repair work. And the few boaters who weren't doing their own work preferred to take it to a shop with an established reputation. Joe was willing to work twenty hours a day, but it made no difference. There was no work for him. Towing the occasional boat that went aground barely paid enough to cover his utility bills. Still he talked confidently to Tom and Amy about how business was slowly picking up—so that they wouldn't worry.

But Joe was desperate. It would be just a matter of time before his creditors would begin to seize his tools and equipment. And although he knew his brother wouldn't pressure him for his money, the thought of not being able to repay it left him with an overwhelming feeling of guilt. The thought of having to tell Amy that he wasn't earning enough money for them to marry, nearly drove him to despair. With each passing day he felt more and more that he was failing the only two people that he loved.

With no business coming in from local people, Joe went farther afield to find work. Some marinas in the towns along the western shore of the Chesapeake provided dockage but didn't undertake major engine repairs. Joe began to visit these marinas every few weeks in the hope that they would subcontract some major overhaul work to him. On one of these visits, a drug runner—he never knew the man's name—overheard him pleading for work. The man approached him as he stood alone on a pier, engrossed in thoughts about his money problems. He offered Joe a large sum of money to make a drug pickup on the Bay. At first Joe was going to refuse, but then he thought, *It's the only way I'm going to be able to repay Tom, and besides if I don't do it, someone else will.*

Joe used some of the money he was paid for the first drug run to repay part of his debt to Tom. He spent most of the remainder on several used engines which he rebuilt and sold. The rebuilt engine sales made it seem to Tom and others that Joe's business was beginning to prosper. By the time he had completed his third run, Joe had earned enough money to pay off his debt to Tom completely and his resale of rebuilt engines began to establish his reputation in the marine business. The final drug run, that he was making on this night, would give him plenty of working capital for his business and more than enough money for him and Amy to set a wedding date.

Joe was roused from his thoughts by the rumble of engines. He heard the druggers' boat long before he saw it looming out of the darkness. It was one of the largest cigarette boats he had ever seen. He and Tom had watched similar boats race on the Bay. They were long and narrow, their speed was awesome. This boat was black. As it approached, Joe flashed his running lights three times and shut off his engine as he had been instructed. Someone on the cigarette boat called out to him, but he couldn't hear his instructions because of the noise of the boat's four enormous engines. Then someone aboard the big boat shut off its engines and, except for the lapping of the waves, the night became very quiet. A voice called out softly, "Start your engine and come alongside."

The transfer, about forty kilos of cocaine, was made quickly. One of the druggers, who was carrying some kind of automatic weapon, said tersely, "The Coast Guard has been following us. Get away from here. We'll decoy him away from you." As he shoved off from the big boat Joe said, "Do you think you can lose him? He'll have radar." The drugger laughed, "Nothing on this Bay is fast enough to catch us." As he said this the roar of boat engines could be heard rapidly approaching. Then the beam of a powerful searchlight pierced the darkness and began searching in their direction. The cigarette boat's engines began to rumble again and it moved away slowly in the direction of the light.

Joe started his small engine with the silencer and steered his boat in the opposite direction. From a distance of several hundred yards, he saw the cigarette boat move into the beam of the searchlight. A voice on a loudspeaker identified the third boat as a US Coast Guard vessel and then said, "Stop your engines and prepare to be boarded." Almost instantaneously the cigarette boat leapt forward with a roar so loud that Joe at first thought the boat was exploding. Without hesitation the Coast Guard boat thundered off in pursuit.

Joe immediately shut off his small engine, started his inboard and headed for the Virginia shore at full throttle. After running for about fifteen minutes, he throttled his engine back to an idle. In the far distance he could still hear the two big boats. Both still seemed to be running at top speed. He pushed his throttle ahead again and ran to the west until he could see the outlines of buildings along the shoreline and his depth sounder indicated that he was in only a few feet of water. The beach appeared to be several hundred yards away.

Joe slowed and shut down his engine. Moving back to the transom, he made sure the silencer was still firmly in place over the outboard motor. He started it and left it idling. He knew the Coast Guard men were capable of tracking him on their radar, even as they continued their pursuit of the cigarette boat. He also knew how to make their job a lot more difficult.

Joe reached down and fully inflated the cheap plastic raft that covered the packets of cocaine on his deck. Then he inserted a six-foot aluminum pole with a radar reflector into a holder at each end of the raft. This done, he threw the raft overboard, watched it drift away for a moment, and then motored closer inshore.

When Joe had decided to run drugs with his boat, he removed all of its exterior metal parts to make radar detection more difficult. Even the cleats for his docking lines were made of wood. His radar training in the National Guard had made him aware that certain materials and shapes increased or decreased the amount of radar energy reflected from targets; that was why he had made the silencer for the outboard in the shape of a sphere. He knew that the raft with its reflectors would show up brightly on the Guard's radar screen, and he hoped it would be mistaken for his boat as he motored quietly back to Bayberry Creek. He knew he had a good chance of pulling it off because all the houses and docked boats along the shore would show up as clutter on a radar screen. And if he traveled slowly, as close to the shore as possible, the radar operators would have difficulty identifying his boat in all of that clutter.

Joe made it back to Bayberry Creek without being caught by the Coast Guard. He never knew whether it was because of his precautions or because they simply chased the cigarette boat until they were out of radar range.

Back at his building on the creek, he unloaded the cocaine and placed it in a box between some outboard engines that were sitting on dollies. Then he made a phone call to a number he had been given, let the phone ring twice and hung up. Finally, to make things look normal, he remounted the towing tripod on his boat and removed the silencer and GPS. The prearranged pickup time for the drugs was six the next morning.

Joe had taken much longer to get back from the drug rendezvous than it had taken him to get there. Still, it was not quite 11:00 PM. He had not experienced such tension since the Gulf War, and now that he was safe, he was physically and mentally exhausted. As he lay down on an old cot in the back of the shop he remembered what he had forgotten to do. He hadn't told Tom that he wouldn't be coming home tonight. But before he could comprehend the implications of that thought, he was in a deep, almost coma-like, sleep.

Joe was awakened by a soft knocking on the door. He looked at the wall clock. It was 6:00 AM. When he opened the door, Joe saw the familiar face of the drugger who usually picked up the cocaine from him. He could see his late model van behind him with its back doors open. The guy was young, perhaps nineteen or twenty. His leather jacket was unzipped; Joe could see a pistol with a silencer in a holster near his left shoulder. He carried two empty duffel bags in his left hand and a cheap briefcase in his right hand. He chuckled, "Heard you guys ran into some trouble last night. Those Coast Guard jerks never learn. Here's your money, where's the stuff?" He handed Joe the briefcase as Joe pointed to the box between the outboard motors.

The drugger began removing the cocaine from the box and packing it in the duffel bags. Joe opened the briefcase and counted his money. The drugger stopped several times during the packing and looked around. It was a big haul and he was very nervous. Joe thought, *I'd better tell him now, that this was my last run.* But before he could utter a word the door opened and Tom stepped into the room.

Tom looked at Joe, "Where were you last..." He never finished the sentence. The drugger, in one motion, swung around from his kneeling position next to the duffel bags, pulled his gun and fired. The gun made a soft crack. Tom fell to his knees with his hand pressed to a rapidly reddening spot in the center of his work shirt. Then with a soft moan, he pitched sideways onto the floor. Joe was at his side as he hit the floor. As he picked him up in his arms, he knew his brother was dying.

The drugger raced from the room with the duffel bags. In a moment he was back, wheeling one of the outboard motors out of the door. Then he was back again, taking another motor. Joe knelt next to Tom, trying to stop the blood flowing from his chest. He heard the back doors slam on the van. The drugger stuck his head in the door, "I'm taking two of your motors. Tell the police the guy walked in on a robbery, and you'll be in the clear." He pointed at the briefcase with the money, "There's plenty more where that came from. I'll be in touch." Joe barely heard him, he was dialing the phone. Within minutes an ambulance was on the way. Joe rode to the hospital in the ambulance with Tom and called the sheriff's department from there.

Amy arrived at the emergency room thirty minutes later. Several deputies were talking quietly in a corner. They told Amy that Tom had died just minutes before her arrival and that they had called her at Joe's request. As is often the case in small rural communities, the two deputies knew Tom and Joe personally. They were reluctant to interrupt Joe's grieving, but they told Amy that they had to get a statement from him as soon as possible. So far, they only knew that Tom had been shot, nothing more. Amy asked to have a few minutes to console Joe before they took his statement.

Amy found Joe sitting on a chair in an adjoining room, with his elbows on his knees and his head in his hands. She sat beside him and put her arms gently around him. He raised his head, and she saw a look of pure agony on his ashen face. He looked down into his hands and said, "Tom's dead. All I ever wanted was you, and for Tom to be proud of me." Then quietly he told her every detail of what had occurred that night. Everything that had been done, every word that had been spoken.

As the story was told, Amy's expression changed from one of disbelief to profound sorrow. Great tears rolled down her cheeks as she silently cried. When at last Joe was silent, she said, "What will we do now? What will you do? Tom would not want you to throw your life away."

Joe said, "I've killed my brother."

Through the glass in the door Amy could see that the deputies were growing impatient. Joe turned his head and looked directly at Amy. There was a deep sadness in his eyes. He kissed her softly on the lips, stood, and walked slowly over to the door where the deputies were waiting.

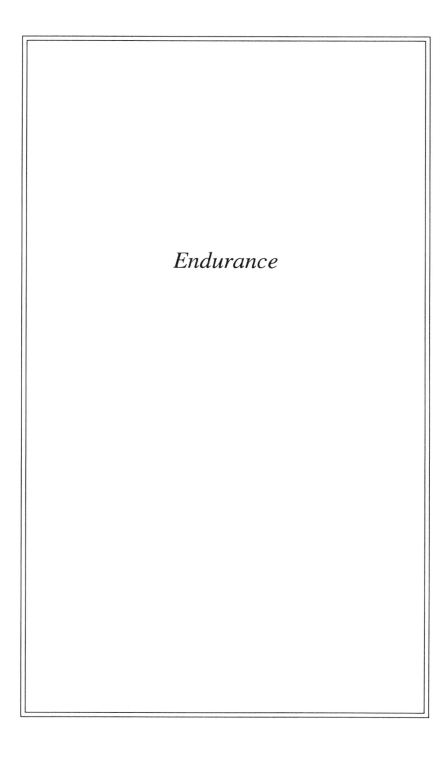

Endurance

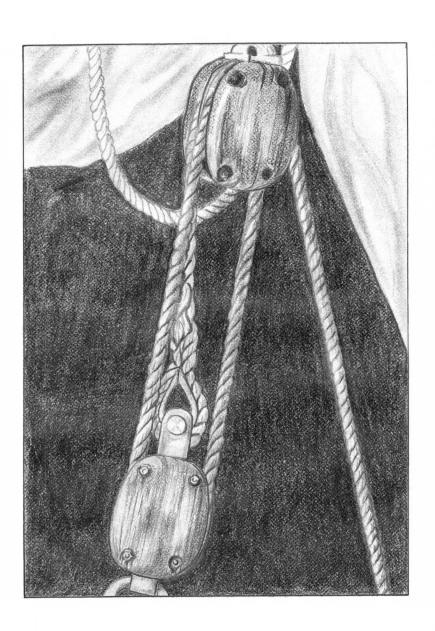

Endurance

The little cutter rocked restlessly in her slip in Bayberry Creek. Although the weather turned warm the day before, it had been a cold October on the Chesapeake, and the temperature was beginning to drop again. Sam looked up from the deck at the small puffy white clouds scudding across a crystal blue sky, and without looking at the masthead indicator, he knew that the wind had shifted from west to northeast.

He had been working doggedly for forty-five minutes on a knot in a block and tackle. It was a special rig that he used to use with a bosun's chair to haul himself up the mast. At sixty he was farsighted and twice he nearly gouged himself with the marlinspike as he tried to break the grip of the rock-hard knot. Grudgingly, it finally came free. After a brief pause he carefully coiled the line, then with some difficulty he lifted the heavy lid off a mahogany deck box and stowed the rig. His back ached and his fingers were sore from tugging on the nylon tackle.

Sam stood and worked the stiffness out of his stocky frame while his brown eyes roamed slowly over *Endurance*, the second love of his life. Under their protective blue covers the mainsail and staysail were neatly folded on their booms, and the jib was snug in its bag in the bow pulpit. In the mid-afternoon sunshine the decks almost glowed with the warm tan color of recently sanded and oiled teak. They had equipped *Endurance* with bronze fittings in the fall of 1947. Sam never regretted that decision. Now, ten years later, the heavy winches, chainplates and turnbuckles and the massive cleats for the ground tackle showed no signs of wear and only the slightest tinge of green from the salt air. Indeed, they seemed to emphasize how well the boat had been constructed. Sam sighed, "I should be in half as good a shape." The boat had been the only thing of any interest to him since Mary died, two years ago. He was adjusting a spring line for added protection against the increasing wind when, out of the corner of his eye, he caught a movement.

Turning, he saw Jenny Moore. She held her right hand out in front of her for protection as she tried to hurry through the swaying holly and dogwood that lined the small path she was following down the hill from her cottage. As she approached the creek, she used her left hand to protect her eyes as small wind dervishes, full of beach sand, whirled about her. Sam stepped onto the dock and called out to her, "Move off the path, away from the bank, back into the pines, it'll be easier going." She turned abruptly and as she headed into the pines, he lost sight of her. Jenny and her husband John were his nearest neighbors and he and Mary had taken a liking to them.

The Moores' cottage was just a few hundred yards from his, where Bayberry Creek made an abrupt turn into the Bay. Their cottage, like his, was a vacation retreat, and had three medium-size rooms, a bedroom, a combination kitchen, dining, living area, and a screened-in porch. The amenities were few. The cottage had electricity, an oil stove for cool fall evenings and an old refrigerator. There was no telephone. In the kitchen area, a cast-iron hand pump, painted with bright red anti-rust paint, provided the water that they used for washing. The well-water was slightly salty and they hauled large carboys of fresh water from the village for drinking. Occasionally they hauled water for Sam, since he did not keep a car at his place, fearing the salt air would damage its paint.

Sam had dined with the young couple the previous evening. He remembered that he had wanted to turn down the dinner invitation, but he couldn't come up with a good enough excuse. In the end, he was glad he didn't. The dinner had been simple—a platter piled high with crab cakes, a bowl of cold slaw, home-made bread, and an inexpensive white wine. Dessert had been peach cobbler, purchased from the village bakery. In earlier days, he and Mary had shared many similar meals, but it was his first wholesome dinner in a week.

Later, they sat on the squeaky old swing out on the porch and drank the last of the wine. As the wind made a soft swishing sound in the loblollys outside the screens, the three of them talked about the Bay and John's plan to sail to Heron Island in the morning. John had a small catamaran and was a good, if somewhat inexperienced, sailor. According to him, his little twin-hulled "cat" fairly flew across the water. Jenny was uncomfortable on a boat that always seemed poised to "take off" and preferred a beach chair and a good book. He didn't know why, but the obvious affection between the two young people made Sam feel good, and a little envious. Something in Jenny's manner reminded him of his Mary. Before Mary's death the two had been close friends. Jenny's call, "Sam," brought him back to the present.

Sam looked at Jenny as she hurried down the dock. He hardly noticed her disheveled appearance, the scratches from the holly, her labored breathing. What riveted his attention was the look in her eyes. He had seen it only once before. He and Mary had been caught in a gale, the boat broached, he had been thrown across the cockpit into the lifelines and had nearly gone overboard. He remembered seeing that same look of fear in Mary's eyes as she watched him struggle to stay on board. He knew something was very wrong. Jenny blurted out, "Sam, John is still out on the Bay. He should have been back by now!"

In the few minutes that followed the whole story came out in a rush. That morning John had pushed his catamaran down the grassy creek bank and headed out into the Bay for Heron Island. He had wanted her to go with him, but she had a book she wanted to finish before their vacation ended. Besides, their car was in the village garage for brake work, and she expected the mechanic to deliver it to the cottage sometime that afternoon. She would have to be there to pay the man when it arrived. According to the morning radio broadcast, a high was moving toward the Bay, but it wasn't supposed to arrive before dark. It was now after 3:00 P.M. John hadn't returned. The mechanic hadn't brought the car. The sky and the wind gave every indication that they were about to be hit by a Nor'easter. And she had no way of calling for help.

Jenny looked at him and said, "Sam, can we take your boat and go look for him?" It was a plea rather than a question. Sam shook his head slowly, "With her small engine I don't know if she can make it through the waves at the creek mouth." Jenny looked straight into his eyes and said, "Sam, please." Mary used to say the same words. Sam said, "Jenny, I'll find him. Go back to your cottage. As soon as the mechanic brings your car, go to the village and call the Coast Guard, tell them everything."

Sam boarded *Endurance* and hurried forward to the bowsprit where the anchors sat in their chocks. He knew he had to lighten the bow if the boat was going to make it through the waves at the creek mouth. With his rigging knife he cut the nylon rode from the medium-sized Danforth. He threw the anchor onto the dock, stuffed the unraveling end of the rode down its hawse pipe and secured the pipe cover. The big plow anchor was more of a problem because it had a chain rode. He released the plow from its chocks and dropped it into the creek. Pulled by its own weight, nearly one hundred feet of chain followed the anchor to the bottom until with a dull thud the bitter end jerked up against the post to which it was fastened below deck.

Sam ran aft and plunged down the main hatch into the cabin. Moving forward, he gave each of the latches on the bronze portholes and the forward hatch a hard twist to be sure they were dogged down. With a jerk he opened the chain locker and with a single stroke of his rigging knife sliced through the line that secured the bitter end of the anchor chain to the boat. With grim satisfaction, he saw the end of the chain run up through the chain pipe, and heard it fall into the water. He could retrieve it later. On his way aft through the cabin he grabbed a life jacket, his safety harness and a pair of sailing gloves.

Back on deck, Sam started the engine, and while it was warming up he ran forward again. After replacing the cover on the chain pipe he ripped the covers off both the mainsail and the staysail and threw them on the dock. Working quickly, he put double reefs in both sails. He didn't intend to use the cutter's third sail, the yankee jib, so he unfastened it from the forestay fitting and threw it bag and all onto the dock. Back in the cockpit he recoiled the throwing line attached to the life ring and replaced it in its holder. He put on his life jacket and harness, took one last look around and decided that he was ready. He cast off the dock lines and eased *Endurance* out of the slip into the creek.

As the boat motored toward the final bend in the creek, Sam checked the wind. At that point the strip of land that separated the creek from the Bay was less than a hundred yards wide. The shoreline was heavily forested with Virginia and loblolly pine and below the pine branches, holly, dogwood and bayberry formed an almost impenetrable barrier to the wind. But looking at the wildly swaying tree tops, he knew it must be blowing at least twenty-five to thirty knots on the Bay.

Sam brought *Endurance* to a stop and uncleated his main and staysail sheets. Then he went forward and raised his sails. When he returned to the cockpit he snapped the shackle on the end of his harness to an eye bolt. He could not see the Bay yet, but he watched the rollers coming into the creek where it made its turn into that broad expanse of water. Every sixth or seventh roller was larger than the rest. As he approached the bend, he could feel the boat lifting rhythmically as each incoming wave caused a surge in the creek. He was very near the bend now. Seeing a large wave rushing past from the creek entrance, he pointed his bow just aft of it and jammed the throttle full ahead. As the rpm needle entered the red area on the gauge, the two pistons in the small engine began to make a dull knocking sound, like a hammer striking a piece of soft wood. The knotmeter showed four knots. The cutter was a double-ender and heavy for her length. She wasn't built to race, she was built to cruise under sail, to endure, and to protect her crew. Sam and Mary had always had great confidence in her.

At the bend the creek turned almost ninety degrees and headed due east into the Bay. The wind was now out of the northeast, and Sam knew he would be fighting both it and the waves as he clawed his way out of the creek. He pushed the tiller leeward and, fighting the rolling motion of the incoming waves, brought the boat around in a smooth arc to a position very near the far side of the creek. He was now heading diagonally across the creek, directly into the wind. Just over a hundred yards ahead he could see the red day mark indicating the northern end of the creek entrance. Waves were breaking over the end of the rock jetty on which it sat. The boat's forward progress had slowed to less than two knots. The engine was overheating. He could feel the pounding of its pistons through the thick deck planking, but he couldn't hear it. His ears were filled with the howling of the wind, the crashing sound of the waves as they beat themselves to death on the creek bank, and the whip-cracking sounds of dacron sails trying to flog themselves into strips of rag.

Twice in the hundred yards to the day mark *Endurance* buried her bow in waves that nearly brought her to a dead stop. But the engine forced her slowly onward. Black smoke was beginning to billow out of her exhaust pipe. In that hundred yards Sam winched in the main and staysail sheets. Then, dangerously close to the day mark, the boat rose on the crest of a wave and Sam put the tiller to port. She came about quickly, and almost simultaneously the two sails filled with a boom that shook the entire boat. Two minutes later, with a metallic thud, the engine froze. But *Endurance* was sailing, heeled over with the lee bulwark nearly awash, and clear of the southern rock jetty by a hundred feet. With deep water under keel and both sails drawing the cutter was in her element.

Sam sat in the cockpit, mouth wide open, gasping for breath. Only four or five minutes had elapsed from the time he entered the bend in the creek until he reached his present position, but the muscles of his arms, legs and back were filled with a dull aching, as if he had been chopping green wood for hours. He had forgotten to put on his gloves and the fingers of his left hand were bleeding from fighting the sheets. Beneath his life jacket and foul weather gear he was hot and very sticky, and his heart felt like it was trying to beat its way out of his chest. Being hot didn't bother him. Sitting in the cold wind and spray he knew that the chill would get to him soon enough. But the cold wind reminded him about John. If he was in the water, even with his life jacket on, the exertion, chill wind and cold water would sap his strength quickly.

Sam had been thinking about how to search for John since leaving the dock. *Heron Island is about three miles offshore and a little over six miles down the bay*, he thought. *I'm going to assume he made it to the island and was returning when the wind shifted to the northeast and picked up. I'll head in a straight line for the island, if he tacked west of the line and went overboard, he'll drift southwest. If I don't find him, I'll return on a parallel track closer inshore.*

Sam clenched the tiller in his right hand and locked his left arm around the boom gallows to steady himself. *Endurance* churned along with the wind on her aft quarter, sliding and plunging with a corkscrew motion as overtaking waves lifted and dropped her stern. He squinted his eyes against the salt spray and searched for John. First from the port side of the boat to the horizon and then along the horizon to the bow. Then from the starboard side to the horizon and to the bow. Then back to port, over and over and over. Within twenty minutes he was wet from spray and shivering. His left arm and shoulder ached terribly. He assumed it was from holding onto the boom gallows as the boat went through the corkscrew motions. A feeling of nausea added to his misery. He thought, *it's strange, I've never been sick on the water before, why now, Lord?*

An hour later, as he approached Heron Island, Sam hadn't found John. He knew he was going to have to reverse his course and tack farther to the west. As he came around, he hauled in the sheets of both sails so tightly that the sails were nearly self-tending. Even with both sails double-reefed the boat was heeling dangerously. It took all his strength with both hands on the tiller just to steer. Fifteen minutes after heading upwind he had nearly despaired of finding John. Waves were continually smashing into the bow, and the spray was making it increasingly difficult to see.

Then as he came over the crest of a wave and slammed into its trough he saw the catamaran. One hull was sticking about four feet out of the water and the other was submerged. Its mast was nearly flat on the water, supported there, miraculously it seemed, by the float designed to prevent it from turning over completely. If he had been ten feet farther to port, he would have hit it. As *Endurance* rushed past the half-submerged "cat," he saw John. He was wearing his life jacket and harness and was clinging desperately to the base of the mast.

Sam had practiced a "man overboard maneuver" a dozen times in light winds, and hundreds of times mentally. But never in his wildest imagination did he try to execute the maneuver in a gale. Sam gathered his thoughts and strength, put the tiller to windward and brought the boat around ninety degrees onto a southwest course. He hesitated a few moments and gybed. The boat seemed to come around another ninety degrees in a heartbeat. As the wind caught the back side of the sails, both booms swung across the boat at incredible speed. At the same time a wave caught the aft quarter of *Endurance* and she broached. The ends of both booms plunged into the Bay and water cascaded over the bulwarks into the cockpit. Only his grip on the boom gallows stanchion saved Sam from pitching headlong across the cockpit.

The boat righted itself slowly as water poured overboard through the scuppers and the cockpit drains. Sam checked the compass and brought the boat back on course. It had all happened too quickly to be afraid. Within a few more seconds he went from a broad reach to beating and then he tacked through the wind onto a course that he thought was very close, but slightly downwind, to the one he was running when he saw the catamaran.

Sam had lost all concept of time. Within seconds he was wondering if he had already passed John. But then he saw the cat and John off his starboard bow. He brought the boat up directly into the wind, the sails luffed, and the boat stopped like she had run aground in soft mud. He uncleated the main and staysail sheets. John was no more than fifteen feet to port, but Sam could already feel the boat beginning to drift away. He grabbed the life ring from its holder and threw it with all his strength at a point fifty feet beyond John's head. Instead it landed within inches of his hands and he grabbed it. Sam screamed, "Hold tight, hold tight." Then he crawled forward to the mast on the wildly pitching deck.

The bow had shifted to starboard and the wind was beginning to push *Endurance* away from the cat. Sam released the halyards of both sails. He pulled the mainsail down the mast and left the staysail flapping wildly. He crawled back into the cockpit on his hands and knees. John had gotten his head and shoulders through the life ring and with the last of his strength was holding tightly to the line. *Endurance* was drifting away from the cat, and with each rise and fall of a wave, John was being jerked across the water. Sam braced his feet against the bulwarks and pulled with all his strength, but he could not haul him to the boat.

Sam groaned, "Damn, I've no strength." He blacked out momentarily, but wasn't really aware of it. He recovered in a few seconds, and as his mind cleared he cursed himself for not seeing the obvious. The genoa winch. He took three turns around the winch with the line and slowly began ratcheting John to the boat. Finally, he had John alongside, but he still had to lift his 160 pounds onboard. He tied John's lifeline securely to a mooring cleat and moved forward to the box where he had stored his special block and tackle. He had trouble lifting the heavy cover off of the box and lifting and fastening the block to the boom was almost beyond his strength. He unshackled the bosun's chair and dropped the end of the rig into the water. John snapped its shackle to his safety harness. Once everything was ready, Sam slowly hoisted John onboard. But even with the four-to-one advantage of the block and tackle and the genoa winch, it was a very near thing.

John mumbled only one word as he dropped onto the deck. "Thanks." Sam nodded, he was incapable of responding. Both men lay on the deck and despite the cold neither moved for fifteen minutes. Then, following Sam's instructions, John went below deck and brought up several wool blankets in which they wrapped themselves. Sam was deathly cold and his left shoulder ached like it had been hit by a sledge hammer.

At about this time, back at Bayberry Creek, the mechanic brought the Moore's car. With tires squealing, gravel flying, and the mechanic cringing in the passenger seat, Jenny sped back to the village to raise the alarm. Within two hours Sam and John were found by a Coast Guard cutter, which towed them to a marina just off the Rappahannock river. The seas were too bad for them to attempt a reentry into Bayberry Creek that day.

Jenny arrived at the marina shortly after *Endurance* docked. By now John was recovering his strength. But Jenny was very worried about Sam. His color was ashen and his hands and face were ice cold to the touch. John and Jenny drove him to the hospital. Enroute, Jenny tried to thank Sam for what he had done. Sam was only semi-conscious, but he whispered something in Jenny's ear. A few seconds later they were at the hospital.

In the emergency room the doctors checked Sam thoroughly and decided to keep him in the hospital for a few days. Sam's doctor told Jenny that Sam knew his heart had been deteriorating for some time and that he took an enormous risk going after John. The doctor also said that Sam was totally exhausted, but apparently the ordeal had done no further damage to his heart.

As they drove home from the hospital, John looked at his wife and said, "Jenny the man risked his life for me. Why?" Jenny said quietly, "John, as we were driving Sam to the hospital, I tried to thank him for saving you. He only said, "I did it for Mary."

EPILOGUE

Sam was released from the hospital three days after the rescue. As he convalesced he thought about his boat and the future. He decided that it was time to make a change in his life. The rescue had reminded him of what he already knew, he was a good sailor. And he loved the sea.

As soon as he was able, Sam retrieved *Endurance* from the Rappahannock marina and began taking her out on short cruises. He lost weight and the fresh air and exercise improved his heart condition. He even sailed during the winter months and by the following spring he felt fit and strong. Jenny made sure that he ate regularly and well.

By June, he had fitted-out *Endurance* for extended cruising. Then on a clear and sunny day with a following breeze, he headed south and out of the Chesapeake Bay. In the years that followed, John and Jenny occasionally received letters from Sam. They were mailed from out-of-the-way ports in the Caribbean, Florida and the Gulf Coast. There was still an occasional reference to Mary, but he enjoyed a peace and contentment that was apparent in his writing.

Sam lived nearly sixteen years after his rescue of John. He died peacefully in his sleep aboard *Endurance*. To their surprise, Sam willed the little cutter to John and Jenny. They scraped her bottom clean,

oiled her teak decks and polished her bronze fittings with loving care.
Then like Sam and Mary once did, they set sail together!

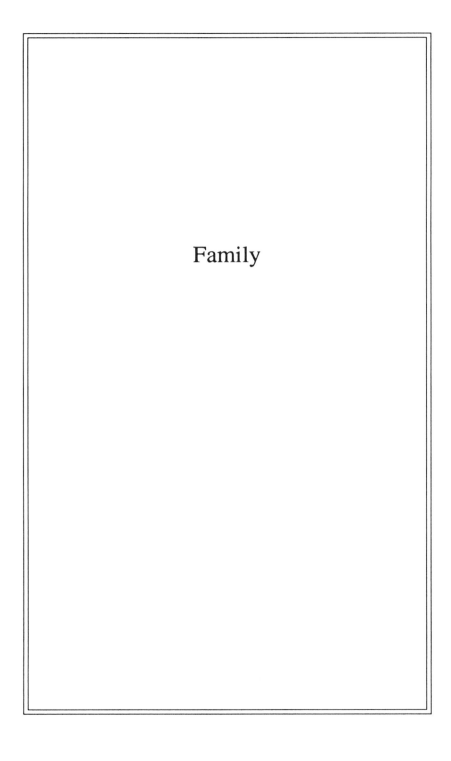

Family

Family

The swing on which Pop was sitting was suspended by rusty chains from the ceiling of the new porch and squeaked softly as he moved. Only Pop called the porch new. Because Zoe had wanted it, he had added it to their house in 1945. Back then, he had worked the oyster beds all day and still had energy left to build the porch—but that was fifty years ago.

Pop had been a waterman on the Chesapeake Bay and its tributaries since boyhood. He was stocky, his shoulders were broad, his large hands protruded from sleeves that always seemed too short, and his fingers were misshapen by years of abuse from chain, wire and rope. Still, when young men shook the old man's hand they could feel the remnants of power in his grip. His full head of hair and bushy eyebrows were white and framed a face that had been weathered by years of labor in the burning sun, the freezing rain, snow, and wind. His eyes were dark and still clear and when he looked at you, you could easily see the joy, the anger, or the love in them.

Pop and Zoe bought the house, known as Aldersly Manor, from the Bonneau family in 1942. The house had been built in the early 1840s by a planter named Geoffrey Aldersly. During the long summer evenings, when he and Zoe were young, they would relax on the front porch and savor the fresh air blowing in from the Bay. Most evenings, just before the sun set they would watch the great blue heron, (whose offspring still roosted nearby), lift into the air above Bayberry Creek and head for the nearby trees that were his home. In the deepening darkness before moonrise, he and Zoe would quietly discuss their dream of the future. Zoe had died in 1992, three years ago, but on warm summer evenings Pop still sat on the porch and talked to her about the dream that they had lived out in the old house.

On this warm June afternoon, Pop sat in the swing and watched his grandson, Tommy. He was ten years old and still had the boundless energy and impatience of a pup. He had auburn hair and brown eyes; eyes which seemed to lighten almost to a golden hue when he became excited. The fact that he was considerably smaller than his friends bothered Tommy a lot. Pop loved him dearly.

Tommy was sitting on Pop's boat dock on Bayberry Creek. He had tied a string to the stern of a homemade toy boat and was trying to make it sail out toward the center of the creek, but each gust of wind hitting the mainsail, however slight, knocked the boat flat. Finally the boy ran back up the dock and jumped down onto the riprap which protected the shoreline. He picked up a large cobblestone and grunting and muttering under his breath, lugged it out to the end of the dock and set it down. Then, he positioned the toy boat so that it floated directly below the edge of the dock. He picked up the cobblestone and with the cry "Bombs away!" dropped it directly on the boat, smashing it to pieces.

"Tommy, come here," Pop called. The boy looked up, saw his grandfather and came bounding up the hill from the creek. He threw himself onto the floor of the porch, leaned his back against the railing and looked at Pop expectantly. Pop stopped swinging. "What are you doing down there, Tommy?"

Tommy sighed. "I was testing my new boat. It wasn't worth a darn. Kept tipping over. I'm going to finish last in the race again." Pop smiled to himself. Tommy's friends had given him a real ribbing last year after his boat had done poorly in the Fourth of July model boat race.

Pop put on his serious face and looked directly at the boy. "Well I know a bit about boats, Tommy, maybe I could help you. I could show you what to do and you could build a new boat in my work shop." Pop knew more than a bit about boats, having worked aboard skipjacks for nearly forty years and powerboats another twenty.

Tommy jumped to his feet. "All riiiight!, we'll build the biggest and fastest boat they've ever seen Grandpa!"

Pop frowned. "We'll try to make your boat the fastest Tommy, but it probably won't be the biggest. And you'll have to do the actual building, otherwise it wouldn't be fair."

Tommy thought about this for a minute. He wanted a big boat, bigger than his big friends had, but he tried not to show his disappointment. Then he had another, more disturbing thought. He looked at the old man. "Mom says you have to move away from here, to a condominium, or in with us. Will we be able to get the boat built before you move? We don't have a workshop at our house."

Pop looked over at his workshop. "I'm not going to be moving Tommy, but the fourth of July is only two weeks off. We'll start work on your boat tomorrow."

Before the two boat builders could make any further plans, they heard a car horn honk. It was Tommy's mother, Jean, come to take him home to Kilmarnock. Tommy's father was a storekeeper, and they lived in town. Pop could not look at his daughter, Jean, without thinking of Zoe. The physical resemblance between mother and daughter was not strong, but they shared a common set of mannerisms; the way they smiled, the way they walked, the soft way they spoke. Pop loved his daughter, but her concern about him was irritating. He knew he was getting old, but he could still take care of himself and if he couldn't take care of the house the way he did when Zoe was alive, it was his problem and his business. Jean worried too much.

As Jean walked over to her father and son, she looked at the two closely. They resembled one another in so many ways. Her son's auburn hair came from her husband's side of the family, but his smile, infectious laughter and his love of boats and the water came from her father's genes. She thought, *he's also going to be short like his grandfather and there's something about him that reminds me of mom too, but I'm not sure what it is.*

As she neared the old waterman and the would-be boat builder she continued to study her father. *He looks tired. He looks thinner. I wonder if he has been eating right? And look at the house, it could use a coat of paint. I wonder if he's thought to check the condition of the furnace? He needs to do that this summer before the weather turns cold.*

As she walked up to her father she said, "Dad, have you...."

But Pop didn't let her finish the question. "Jean don't start in on me. I'm fine. The house is fine. Everything is fine. Tommy and I are going to build a model sailboat. Aren't we Tommy?"

Tommy was all smiles. "Yeah Mom, Grandpa is going to show me how and I'm going to build it. I'm going to win the model boat race this year. We're going to start building it tomorrow!"

The following day Pop gave Tommy two blocks of white pine. Then he showed him how to use a miter box and some small saws to cut away the excess wood. Once that was done he showed Tommy how to trace the lines of the boat on the remaining block of wood and taught him how to use the chisels, carving knives and sanding blocks. The white pine was light and soft and once Tommy started to carve and sand he made rapid progress. At the end of the second day he showed Pop the hull form he had carved. Pop tried to be as gentle as he could when he pointed out the flaws in the hull to Tommy, but below the boat's waterline the hull was not symmetrical and he knew that it would not sail well. When he said that they would have to start over, it was more than Tommy could bear. In frustration he threw down his tools and ran from the work shop so that Pop would not see the tears in his eyes. Pop could hear his bicycle tires crunching on gravel in his driveway as the boy raced for home.

Pop went into his house, phoned his daughter and invited himself to dinner. Tommy was unusually quiet at the dinner table that evening. After they had finished their meal and cleared off the table, Pop said he had something to show them. He had left a shopping bag by the back door when he arrived. He brought it to the table where they were sitting and spilled out its contents.

The pictures which fell from the bag covered nearly half of the table top. There were dozens of them, and in each one a sailboat could be seen. There were pictures of the bow of the boat, the stern, cockpit, foredeck and of the keel. There were even pictures from the top of the mast looking down on the deck. Many of the pictures also contained an image of a woman. In some of the pictures she was young, in others middle aged, and in still others, older. Jean stared at her father in amazement. "Why it's Mom and our boat the *Zoe Marie*! Dad when did you ever take all these pictures?" Pop said nothing.

Tommy, holding a picture of the stern of the boat on which the name *Zoe Marie* could be clearly seen, looked at his grandfather and said, "Zoe Marie, wasn't that Grandma's name?" Pop smiled and said, "Yes it is."

Pop explained to Tommy that the model boat they were trying to build was a small copy of the *Zoe Marie*. Using the pictures he explained to Tommy where "they" had made carving mistakes and how he and Tommy could correct them on the next block of wood.

Tommy went to bed eager for the next day to come so that he could start to work again on his sailboat. Afterward Pop and Jean and Jean's husband John talked about the good times they had on the old *Zoe Marie*. Pop explained in detail to John how he had built the boat. And he told Jean for the first time that her mother had convinced him to sell the boat so that they would have enough money to send her to college. Jean had always known that her parents loved her, but she also knew how they had loved that boat too, and she was very moved by the story.

At the evening's end, Jean and John made one more attempt to convince Pop that he should move in with them. She thought she saw him waver when she said that he was a good influence on Tommy and that Tommy would love to have him live with them. But when Pop said that he would never leave Zoe's house, Jean realized that moving out of that house was probably the only thing that her father would never do for her. For a moment a thought crossed her mind. *What if we were to move in with him?* Then she remembered how often she had heard her husband say how convenient it was to be able to walk to work from their house in town. *No*, she thought, *it would be too much to ask of John.*

Over the next ten days Tommy and Pop built the sailboat. There were other setbacks. Tommy almost rebelled when he had to sand the bottom of the hull a fifth time and put on a sixth coat of varnish. And, as he watched, Pop thought that installing the small movable centerboard and rudder would have tried even his patience. But the boy did it and his grandfather couldn't wait to show off the boat to the boy's father.

Tommy said that his boat would be the only one with a movable rudder and tiller and centerboard. And Pop said, "that may work to your advantage." Then he taught Tommy to sail the boat and how to adjust the rudder and centerboard for different tacks and wind conditions. Of course, they named the boat the *Zoe Marie*.

On July 4th, the day of the race, the winds were light but steady on Indian Creek. It seemed to Tommy that half of the people in Kilmarnock had come down to the cove near the old steamboat landing to see the model boats race. The boats were to sail straight across the cove to the finish line where some adults in dinghies would retrieve them and return them to their owners.

They raced in heats. In the first two heats, the judges divided the boats by size and *Zoe Marie* won easily. However, in the final heat, when he saw that his friends' boats were all at least twice as large as his, Tommy's confidence plummeted. Some of the other boys even snickered when they saw how small his boat was compared with theirs. But then Pop walked up to him and said. "The wind is changing, mind your tiller and centerboard setting. And remember, it's not how big they are, it's how good they are. And that goes for people as well as boats."

Tommy licked his finger and held it up over his head to judge the wind direction. He knew his boat had a weather helm and that the wind was strong enough to make his boat head up into it and slow it down or maybe even make it stop, so he adjusted his sails, tiller and centerboard so that they would help keep his boat on course.

As he waited for the starter's pistol to fire, he held the *Zoe Marie* by the stern. The wind tugged at his hair and the little boat tried to pull loose from his hand. *Boy,* he thought, *she really wants to go. Grandpa was right, size doesn't mean a thing.* Then the gun went off. *Zoe Marie* heeled over dangerously for a second and then, as her lead centerboard forced her mast upright, she began to move forward. At first she moved slowly, but then she heeled just slightly, and began to move faster, and faster. She sailed straight for the finish line across the cove.

There were six boats in the final heat and most of them did not fare as well. The wind knocked two down within ten feet of the starting line. Two others made it nearly half way across the cove, then they rounded up into the wind, took off on the opposite tack and were knocked flat by the wind. The sixth boat, *Valiant* ran neck and neck with *Zoe Marie* for three quarters of the way across the cove. Then the wind picked up just a little more. She was a big boat, nearly three times the size of Tommy's. She carried a lot of sail and slowly, with her bow still pointed at the finish line she began drifting sideways downwind. She was sailing as fast as *Zoe Marie* but the downwind drift made all the difference. *Valiant* passed outside of the finish line marker and was disqualified. To the enthusiastic cheering of the crowd *Zoe Marie* crossed the finish line first with the nearest boat fifty feet behind.

Tommy screamed, "Yes, Yes, Yes!" and, in imitation of his father, did what only can be described as an Indian war dance. Jean clapped and clapped and clapped. Pop just smiled and tussled Tommy's hair.

Jean made a victory dinner that evening. They had Tommy's

favorite, chicken pot pie. It was Pop's favorite dinner too and this gave Jean one last chance to convince Pop to move in with them. As before, he didn't even let her warm to the subject before he shook his head, "No, No, No!"

Then Tommy grabbed his grandfather's hand and spoke up. "Grandpa can't move here, we're going to build more boats and we need to be near his workshop. Why don't we move in with him?"

Pop beamed, "Not only is he good with tools, he's smart." And turning to Jean he said, "Why not?" Jean turned and looked at her husband.

John looked at her and said, "Why not indeed."

Jean looked at Tommy. *He's got my husband's brains, my father's energy and personality and my mother's heart, but he's my son!* She looked at her father and said, "When would you like us to move in?"

The Neapolitan

The Neapolitan

From ancient times certain women are said to have been born with the gift, (some call it the curse), of the evil eye. Women from the Italian city of Naples (Neopolis) are thought to inherit this gift more frequently than others. The owner of the evil eye has always been particularly feared by the superstitious, especially sailors and fishermen. This is the story of one such woman and the curse she cast upon a commercial fisherman from the Northern Neck of Virginia. It was told to me by an Irishman who married a girl of Italian descent, so I cannot vouch for its authenticity.

Jack Kinney was the kind of man that other men admire. If he was your friend, you could depend on him to be at your side if you needed help fighting a storm at sea or three drunken sailors in a bar. But for a big man, he had a soft voice and his smile, like his nature, was generous. His curly hair was a deep red, nearly auburn. Sometimes a stranger would call him "Curly," but never more than once. Jack was twenty-eight years old and single, but much to the dismay of the local belles around Millenbeck, normally Jack paid little attention to the ladies.

In July 1914, when the events of this story occurred, Jack was a relative newcomer to the Northern Neck. He had moved to the area from Baltimore that spring and worked as a ship's mate on a commercial fishing boat. At the time many of the ships' captains recruited their crews from the men of Lancaster, Northumberland, Richmond and Mathews counties. Jack loved the ocean and the Chesapeake Bay and it seemed to his friends that he was happiest when he was on the deck of a fishing boat.

That summer the menhaden were everywhere in the Chesapeake Bay and along the ocean coast. Jack worked with a good crew on a good commercial ship that netted hundreds of thousands of the oily little fish each day. The daylight temperatures were scorching and he sweated along with the rest of his mates; working the nets, raising and lowering purse boats on their davits, and transferring tons of menhaden from purse nets into the hold of their ship. After working from dawn to dusk for twenty-one days straight, they put into port at Reedville, Virginia for a week's layover. The men needed rest so that strained arms and backs could regain their strength, and hands that had been bruised and cut on the nets could heal.

Being a bachelor with no particular plans for this break, Jack stayed aboard ship for the first four days. He spent the warm summer evenings wandering about Reedville taking in such delights as it offered, which were few indeed for a single man. Then he took the steamer to Millenbeck, which was located near the confluence of the Rappahannock and Corrotoman Rivers, about twenty-five nautical miles away by water. He went directly from the dock to his boarding house where he only stopped long enough to drop off his seabag and remove a note tacked to his door. The note was from his landlady, it reminded him that his rent was overdue. He folded the note neatly, stuck it in his pocket and headed for his favorite drinking hole, Big Henry's place down by the waterfront.

As he entered the door of the drinking establishment, Jack saw two of his friends sitting at a table and two locals standing at the bar. Years earlier the building that the bar occupied had been an oyster shucking house. There were few windows and the interior was dark and cool. As he walked across the room his feet kicked up small clouds from the dirt and sawdust on the floor. He looked at Big Henry standing behind the bar, his massive back reflected in the round mirror behind him. He was breaking up a fifty-pound block of ice with a screwdriver and carefully placing the fragments around bottles of beer sitting in a washtub. The mirror behind Big Henry's rough-hewn oak bar came from a woman's vanity dresser. He had retrieved it from a local dump.

66

Bottles of bourbon, scotch, and gin lined a small counter in front of the mirror. Big Henry carried no cognac, wines, or liqueurs. His was a workingman's bar. A woman had never entered the place, not even his wife. Nor would one want to, considering its condition.

As Jack approached his friends he called to Big Henry, "A round of draft here and for the boys at the bar. They're on me. And bring some of those hard-boiled eggs." Jack drank draft beer, rather than bottled stuff, whenever he could. He thought the latter to be too gassy. One of the men at the table laughed. "Spoken like a true friend and single man, Jack." Jack's friends were married and had little extra cash to spend on drinking. He had no family; no wife, no children, and no parents. He sometimes thought about getting a dog for company, but what would he do with it when he was aboard ship for weeks at a time? Tonight he wouldn't be drinking alone and he had three weeks pay in his pocket.

The two men seated at Jack's table were also fishermen. One, whose name was Tony, worked with Jack. The other, Alex, worked on a different boat. Once they had their beer and hard-boiled eggs, they began to talk about fishing. They agreed amongst themselves that the season was going well. Alex said that he heard that all the other boats in the fleet were bringing in holds filled with fish too. Tony added that he thought catches during the remainder of the season would also be good. The three men nodded. Then with real concern, realizing that they had tempted fate, all three simultaneously gave three sharp raps on the wooden table top.

The conversation switched to crabbing and the price of a bushel of jumbos. A man couldn't buy a bushel for less than $1.50. Prices were getting out of hand! Jack's friend, Tony, said, "Forget crabs, the Rappahannock is full of eels this year." The others laughed and Jack said, "Only a foreigner would talk of catching and eating eels, when crabs, rockfish, flounder, trout and spot are there for the taking."

Tony (Antonio) was an Italian-American, born in Italy, one of very few in the Northern Neck at that time. He was an extraordinarily good friend to Jack because Jack, who was a powerful swimmer, had saved his life earlier that year when he had been knocked overboard into a raging sea by an errant boom. Jack had leaped into the water and pulled him, unconscious, into a nearby purse boat.

But on this day Jack really didn't want to talk about fishing. "I've a suggestion," he said. "I hear that there's a good comedy, 'The Big Shot', playing over at Irvington, at the James Adams Floating Theater.

What do you say to the three of us going Wednesday night?" The other two men looked embarrassed. They knew their wives would be upset at such an expenditure of family funds, especially if they were not invited. Jack sensed their uneasiness and tried another topic. "Looks like it's going to be Boston and Philadelphia in the World Series again this year." But all three men had talked baseball nearly every evening onboard their fishing boats, and they had tired of that topic.

Big Henry, fearing that the party might break up, cranked up his new gramophone. As the scratching noise from the instrument's horn subsided, the voice of the great Irish tenor John MacCormack filled the bar room. Jack was a passable Irish tenor and he soon joined in with MacCormack. The singing started with "I'll take you home again, Kathleen." Then Big Henry put on "Danny Boy," and followed that with "Galway Bay." Big Henry soon ran out of records, but it made no difference. By this time, others in the bar had joined Jack in singing sentimental Irish melodies. The beer and the tears flowed freely, no matter that Jack was the only Irishman among them.

By now Jack was in a mellow mood. He loved his friends, the beer, Big Henry, and even Big Henry's dog, who was inordinately fond of beer and kept trying to get onto his lap. The drinking finally ended at 2 A.M. None of the crowd, except Jack, had any money. So he paid the tab and Tony, who had a horse and buggy, drove him to his rooming house. It was a dark night and as Jack stepped down from the buggy, Tony handed him a candle lantern.

As he staggered toward the door of the rooming house, a black cat came out from behind the stoop. Jack stamped his foot and yelled a mild profanity at him. Startled, the cat leapt back and stared at the man. The animal looked fat and well-cared for. Even in the flickering candle light, Jack could see its fur glistening. Although the cat looked healthy enough, it had a kink in its unusually long tail.

Since Jack did not believe in tempting fate, he took the steps of the porch two-at-a-time and quickly went into the house before the cat could pass in front of him. He went directly to the door of his room. It was locked. He never locked his door. There was nothing of value in his room, only his seabag with his clothes. Confused, he shook the door handle and heard someone stirring inside. The door opened and a man stood facing him.

The man looked at Jack with sleepy eyes and said, "What can I do for you mate." Jack recognized him. He was a cook from one of the fishing boats. Jack muttered, "You're in my room." The cook yawned, "Sorry mate, you didn't pay your rent and the Neapolitan rented it to me." Jack remembered the note that had been tacked to his door. "Well then cookie, let me get my seabag and I'll be gone." The cook shook his head, "She took it. Goodnight mate." And having said that, he shut the door.

Jack walked out to the barn behind the boarding house, climbed into the hayloft and tried to make himself comfortable. As he lay in the hay, he thought of the Neapolitan. He had talked to her only a few times. Usually the meals he had taken in the dining room of the boarding house had been served by an assistant, while the Neapolitan prepared food in the kitchen. *And fine meals they were too!* he thought.

He remembered from their meetings that she was an unusual woman; tall, dark-haired, with very dark eyes—eyes which, for some reason, he found very disturbing. Several times he caught her looking at him, as if she wanted to ask him a question, but each time she flushed and turned away without saying a word. He remembered feeling disappointed. On one occasion, when she did serve at table, she leaned over Jack to place a platter. She was so near that Jack could feel the warmth of her body and smell the scent of her lilac cologne. He had a nearly uncontrollable urge to reach out and touch her. She seemed to sense something and for once she looked directly at him. He saw his own reflection in her eyes and this time it was he who was embarrassed.

But, Jack thought, *she's a hard woman. Must be a very hard woman, to throw a man out of his room like that. Well, I'll have to deal with her in the morning. I must have my clothes.* With that he fell into an inebriated sleep.

About mid-morning the following day, Jack was awakened by the sound of a horse and buggy leaving the barn. He was hungry, unshaven, dirty, and he itched from the bites of the insects that lived in the hay. Before he could do anything, he needed a change of clothes. So he marched up to the house. He didn't have enough money left to pay the Neapolitan her rent, but he would offer to pay it with interest after the next fishing trip.

He straightened his clothes, brushed his hair back with his hands and knocked on the door to her rooms. No answer. He knocked even louder. No answer. She must not be at home. He tried the door. It was locked. He turned the handle, pushed harder and heard wood break. The door swung open. He had not intended to break the door, but he was a big man and sometimes not aware of his own strength. There, just inside the door, sat his seabag. He took it and left quickly.

Pondering his unintentional crime, he wandered down the dusty street to the waterfront. Later as he sat on the cannery dock watching an osprey making graceful arcs across a cloudless blue sky, he heard a horse approaching. Turning, He saw Tony in his buggy. When Tony heard what Jack had done, he shook his head. "You're welcome to come home with me. I'll feed you and you can clean up. You can even spend the night with us. But the Neapolitan must never know." Jack looked at him in amazement. "You're afraid of her, a woman?" Tony shook his head again. "You were born here in America. You do not understand. The woman is a Jettatore!" Jack said, "What is this Jettatore?" Tony responded very gravely, "She has the evil eye, she will put a curse on you!"

Jack spent the day with Tony, his wife Maria and their children. He enjoyed himself. Maria was a good cook and even washed his clothes with those of her family. In the afternoon he helped Tony pick tomatoes in the family vegetable garden. It was a large garden and after they had collected several bushels more than Maria could put up, they took the extras to the local cannery and sold them. With their new-found riches, Tony suggested that they go to Big Henry's for a couple of beers. Jack thought, *well it's back to the boat in the morning and three more weeks on the water, so why not?*

Having decided not to over-indulge this evening, the two men sat in a corner of Big Henry's slowly nursing their beer. Suddenly, the door to the establishment exploded inward, slammed into the wall with a crash and, combined with the wind the movement created, raised a cloud of dirt and sawdust. Big Henry, who was closest to the entrance and the only one who could see clearly, stared at the person in the doorway for a moment, then fled the room.

Slowly the dirt and dust settled, and there in the sunlight flooding through the doorway stood the Neapolitan, hands on her hips. Her eyes swept the room and settled on Jack. Tony's face turned ashen and he croaked "Jettatore" and began to edge away from the table, his eye on the back door. Jack was not as easily frightened. He stood up and straightened his back, hoping to make himself appear bigger. He drew back his shoulders and crossed his massive arms. The Neapolitan walked purposefully and fearlessly up to him. As she did so, two other customers managed to flee the room. *She is attractive*, Jack thought, *and very angry. I'm in biiiig trouble!* She stood with her face not more than eighteen inches from his, her finely-chiseled nose at the level of his chin. He noticed her ample bosom heaving beneath her close-fitting dress. Her dark eyes seem to rivet him in place. "You cheated me of my rent and you broke into my home! You are a burglar and a thief."

Jack protested, "I stole nothing, I only reclaimed my clothes, which I need to go fishing in the morning. I will pay you the rent and fix........." Before he could finish, her arms which had been resting beside her slim waist flew upward. Her left hand formed a fist which was clutched tightly to her chest. With her right hand, she jabbed him so sharply with a forefinger that he was forced a full step backward. She hissed at him slowly and softly, "I want more than money from you, Irishman!!"

Before he could regain his composure, she spun around and walked toward the door. But she was not finished. Having reached the entrance, she turned to him again. She pointed her right hand at him with two fingers extended. "I have two curses for you. First, you will be cursed in your coming and your going, if you ever visit this den of iniquity again. And the second curse you will learn by and by. But do not worry.....you will not suffer long." Having said this, she shook her fist at him, smiled, turned and disappeared through the door, leaving behind only a slight fragrance of lilac. Jack was dumbfounded. To an Irishman, to be cursed by someone is a terrible thing.

But Jack's discomfort was nothing compared to Tony's. He had not seen him so upset since a mutual friend lost three fingers in a wire windlass. He grabbed Jack by the arm. "We must leave now! Now!" Jack made a show of slowly finishing his beer before heading for the door. But as he stepped over the threshold, he stumbled and fell face down into the dirt. In the distance they heard someone laughing, and someone in the bar muttered, *in your coming and your going.*

Jack and Tony took the steamer from Millenbeck to Reedville the following morning. They arrived in mid-afternoon and went directly aboard their boat. Most of the crew were already there. They were to get underway on the evening tide. To the west clouds could be seen piling up and the wind had shifted to the north. The captain said to Jack, "Looks like we might get hit by an early Nor'easter tonight. Be sure everything is battened down." Jack's shipmates were all experienced sailors and it wasn't long before the boat was made ready for foul weather. While they were waiting for the tide to change, one of the younger crewmen approached Jack. "Jack, have you seen the ship's new mascot?" Without waiting for a reply, he walked around the corner of the pilot house and moments later reappeared with a black cat. The cat was unremarkable except that it had an unusually long tail with a kink in it.

They had been underway only a short time when the storm hit. It struck much earlier than expected. They were headed down the Chesapeake Bay to Cape Hatteras, but their engine started to knock and vibrate as the ship approached Windmill Point at the mouth of the Rappahannock River. They had not traveled more than fifteen miles from Reedville. Fighting the storm with an ailing engine was not worth the risk, so they ran up the Rappahannock River and dropped anchor below Carter's Creek, a few miles from Millenbeck. It was 9 P.M. Looking at Tony, Jack said, "Bad luck." Tony shook his head, "La Jettatore!"

The storm grew steadily worse. They had set their heaviest anchor, but the captain warned all those on watch to keep careful lookout in case it began to drag. They were in twenty feet of water, but only a few hundred yards from shore, and less than that to shallow water. Their boat was 115 feet long, but still it rocked as if it were a cradle. The wind howled and blew with such force that it knocked the tops off the waves and spray flew horizontally across the surface of the river. The rain and spray together nearly blinded the men on watch as they tried to check the anchor lines. If it were not for the scuppers the water would have been ankle deep on the deck. The thunder and lightning were so ferocious that at times it seemed like they were anchored between two giant warships that were determined to sink one another with cannon fire.

Jack had been scheduled for watch duty in the early hours before dawn, so he went to his bunk early that evening.

At about 3 A.M. one of the men on watch came to wake Jack for his turn on the bridge. His bunk was empty and cold. Since the fellow could not be relieved unless his replacement, Jack, reported to the bridge, he started a search. One-half hour later Jack was still nowhere to be found. The captain was awakened. A new search was ordered. As soon as the storm let up, purse boats were put overboard and the waters in the immediate vicinity of the boat were searched by lantern light. By sunrise they had given up hope. Jack was gone without a trace. And as Tony soon discovered, so was their mascot, the black cat.

In the early morning hours, the captain, the ship's engineer and several of the crew rowed a purse boat up Carter's Creek to the shipyard at Weems. There the captain sent word to the sheriff about Jack's disappearance, and the engineer picked up the parts they needed for their steam engine. The engine was repaired in less than two hours and they got underway for Cape Hatteras. Tony was morose. He thought,

after the Jettatore cursed him, I should not have let him come aboard.
As if to confirm his thoughts the weather turned exceptionally fine
within a few hours of Jack's disappearance and stayed that way for the
rest of the trip.

When Tony's boat returned to Reedville three weeks later, he
immediately booked passage on the *Lancaster*, which within an hour,
was steaming for Millenbeck. She arrived there, after several stops
along the way, in the late afternoon.

Tony slung his seabag over his shoulder, ran down the gangplank
and headed for Big Henry's, the one place where there was sure to be
news of Jack. Henry would know if his body had been found. After
that, somehow, he would settle with the Jettatore.

Tony was still walking up the hill from the steamer landing, when
he heard a horse and buggy approaching behind him. A voice called to
him, "Tony." His seabag fell from his shoulder. It was Jack!

"Jack , we thought you had drowned!"

"Geez Tony, it was only a short swim to the shore, even in that
storm!"

Tony was so overjoyed at seeing Jack that it was only at this point
that he noticed who was sitting in the buggy next to his friend. It was
the Neapolitan. The two of them got out of the buggy and walked up to
him. Jack said, "Tony, I want you to meet my wife, Gina."

Tony looked from Jack to the woman and said. "But the curse,
you said he would suffer." He had not realized that the Neapolitan
was a beautiful woman until that moment. She gave him a dazzling
smile. "But he did, I made him suffer quite a while, before I said yes."
Tony clasped Jack's hand, shook it vigorously, hugged him European
style and took him aside and asked, "Everything is all right?" Jack
laughed "Everything is great."

Then Tony grabbed Jack's arm and said, "Tonight we'll go to Big
Henry's and celebrate." Jack pulled his arm free and jumped back.
With a furtive glance at his wife he said, "Do you think I'm crazy?"

EPILOGUE

Jack Kinney never worked on a commercial fishing boat again.
Even if he had wanted to, it is unlikely that any ship's captain would
have hired him. After all, husbands and wives quarrel, and what's to
happen to a captain's boat if such a husband is married to a Jettatore?

Friends

Friends

The wound in his shoulder was not fatal, but the young Confederate lieutenant broke it open repeatedly as he crawled along ditches and fought his way through brambles in the darkness. The wound was a shallow furrow plowed by a minie ball across the uppermost part of his left arm. It oozed blood constantly and made his shoulder stiff and sore and his arm ache all the way to his wrist.

After sneaking through the enemy's lines northeast of Richmond, Virginia, he had walked for seven days in an easterly direction down the center of the Middle Peninsula. Traveling alone and mostly at night, he had thus far avoided farmhouses along the way because he knew that if the Yankees caught him in one, it would go very hard on the family that had sheltered him. But he had slept very little and his strength was failing. As he approached another modest farmhouse on a creek near Mobjack Bay, he knew that he could go no farther without food and rest.

In a wood lot, several hundred yards from the farmhouse, he dug a hole with his bare hands, then removed a set of work clothes from his pack, the type worn by any farmer or oysterman. He stripped to his underwear and put on the work pants. He removed the dressing from his wound, refolded it, placed it back on the wound, and covered it with a bandanna. He put on the work shirt and buried his uniform in

77

the hole. He carried nothing that would identify him. He had buried his uniform with some reluctance, for now if the Yankees caught him, they would treat him for what he was, a spy.

He walked up to the farmhouse and from a distance of about twenty feet looked in through a window. A middle-aged couple were sitting in two easy chairs and a young woman was sitting in a straight-backed kitchen chair, darning socks. The man was smoking a pipe, his wife was reading from the Bible. He staggered up to the front door and knocked.

The man answered the door and asked him what he wanted. He said, "I am an officer in the Confederate Army. I'm being pursued by Yankee soldiers, but I think I have given them the slip for the time being. I am sorry, but I need food and a place to rest. Can you help me?" The man stepped out onto the porch, looked out into the darkness, and listened for a moment. Then he took the lieutenant by the arm and quickly ushered him into the house. When he removed his hand it was covered with blood.

The man and his wife sat the lieutenant down in a chair and immediately went to work on his wound, cutting away the sleeve and shoulder of his shirt, and removing the filthy dressing and the blood-soaked bandanna. The wife saved the unsoiled portions of the shirt, but the remainder along with the bandanna and soiled bandage was burned in the cookstove. It would not do to have bloody material laying about if Yankee soldiers should arrive at their door. As they worked the man introduced himself and his wife and daughter. The couple carefully cleaned the soldier's wound and rebandaged it, while their daughter prepared a meal for him.

Once treatment of the wound was completed, the wife brought the lieutenant a well-worn but clean shirt. It was the summer of 1864 and food was scarce, but the family gave the young lieutenant all he could eat; fried rockfish, corn bread, sweetcorn, tomatoes and bread pudding. The family had two sons fighting with Lee somewhere around Richmond. They prayed to the Lord each night that someone would care for their boys if they were hurt and hungry. The family's name was Thatcher and the head of the family, like so many of the men near the Chesapeake Bay, was both a waterman and a farmer.

The man and his wife set up a cot for the soldier in the kitchen near the back door of the house, so he could make his escape quickly if the Yankees appeared in the vicinity. But it seemed that the enemy soldiers had lost his trail, and that he was safe for awhile. The exhausted young soldier slept through the night and until mid-afternoon of the following day. Upon waking, he appeared to be much improved and the family asked him many questions about the progress of the war. The answers were all discouraging. In the evening the soldier talked to the daughter. The two were close in age and the young man told her his story.

He was born in Virginia, on a large farm in the southernmost part of the Shenandoah Valley. His father died a few years before the start of the war. His mother, never a strong woman, had serious medical problems and they moved temporarily to Washington D.C. so that she could be treated by a renowned physician who practiced there. After a year or so, when it appeared that war was inevitable, he returned home but she remained behind for treatment. He had made many friends in the capital and knew the city well.

He surprised the young woman by telling her that he thought that the war was wrong from the start, that bloodshed was not the way to solve the country's problems. But once the fighting started, he thought that he must fight to defend friends and home.

As she held his hand, he told her that he had fought in the Seven Days Battle at Fredericksburg, The Wilderness, and in many other battles. He was sickened by all the killing. He spoke softly of the rows of his own men who lay dead after the battles, and of hearing the cries of the wounded Yankees whose officers sent them charging against fortifications they could not possibly take. When he learned that they needed couriers and spies to travel into the north, he jumped at the opportunity to avoid killing more of his fellow man.

The young woman asked, "Does your mother know what you are doing?" He answered, "No. And even when I am in Washington, I dare not visit her. But I have a very close friend who sees her regularly and reports on her health to me. We are like brothers. When I get to the Eastern Shore, he will meet me and see to my safety."

At dinner that evening Mr. Thatcher said to the soldier, "Emily has told us about your mission. We will do what we can to help you to get to the Eastern Shore. I suppose you cannot tell us your name?" The soldier smiled. "No, I cannot tell you my name. But I shall never forget yours and your kindness to me, and if I survive this war I shall return here." He looked at their daughter when he said this. She blushed deeply.

Early the next morning a friend came to the house and told them that Yankee soldiers were in the nearby village of Mathews searching for a Confederate officer, whom they suspected of being a spy. The man had come to warn them so that they might hide their food and valuables. He frowned, "The Yankees are not above requisitioning a few supplies for their war effort."

As soon as the man left, Mr. Thatcher hurried into the kitchen and said to his wounded guest, "The Yankees will probably be here shortly. You'll be safer here than on the road. We'll get you to Gwynn's Island tonight and maybe as far as the Eastern Shore tomorrow night. But for now, I have a hiding place for you."

The young soldier followed Mr. Thatcher out the back door of the house and down to his dock on the creek. The dock paralleled the creek for about fifty feet and its decking extended back to the creek bank. Planking went straight down into the water on the creek side of the dock to protect the shoreline underneath from erosion. The dock appeared no different from hundreds of others that could be found on the dozens of creeks off Mobjack Bay. But there was a difference.

Mr. Thatcher led the lieutenant about two-thirds of the way down the dock and there he pried up two deck boards, exposing a box underneath. The box measured about six and one-half feet by two feet. The bottom was only inches above the high tide line. It had a soft oilcloth cover to keep out the rainwater which might otherwise drip through the deck planking above. The box contained two large smoked hams. These were quickly removed. Mr. Thatcher smiled, "You should be safe here, it has fooled the Yankees before." The lieutenant slipped into the box, Mr. Thatcher replaced the planks and walked back up to the house carrying the hams. The Yankees were pounding on his front door within the hour.

The burly sergeant who stood on the porch was brusque. "We have surrounded your house, give up the man you're hiding and you may get out of this with your life!" Mr. Thatcher thought the sergeant was bluffing.

"There's no one here but my wife and daughter. What gave you the idea that we're hiding someone?" The sergeant shoved him back as far as his front door. "I'll tell you why I know you're hiding him. We found his bloody uniform buried in yonder wood lot!" Mrs. Thatcher heard the conversation from where she stood inside the house and turned white with fear. Mr. Thatcher, angered by the shove, stood his ground. "Well you're wrong, whoever buried that uniform was probably just going down the road to the river. If you don't believe me, search the house, search the barn, search my boat, search everything! I don't give a damn!"

"I'll do just that," said the sergeant. Then telling his men to remain where they were, he walked around the house and down onto the dock, with Mr. Thatcher trailing behind. The two men stood on the dock alone. The sergeant looked up and down the creek and then at Mr. Thatcher.

"The man apparently is not in uniform. That makes him a spy. If I find any sign of him, even a single drop of blood, I'll tell you what I'm going to do. I'll recommend that they hang you. I'll burn your house down, and your barn, and your boat. I'll kill all your livestock, except the chickens which I'll carry off. You'll be dead and your wife and daughter will be destitute. Now for the last time what do you know about Johnny Reb?" Mr. Thatcher shook his head. "I know nothing." The sergeant yelled to his men standing up by the house. "Search everything carefully."

Mrs. Thatcher and Emily were now standing by the back door. As two soldiers started down the path toward the dock, Emily called after them in a concerned voice. "Watch out for the copperheads they're particularly bad this year." She had never known a city boy, and most of these Yankees were city boys, who wasn't scared to death of snakes. The two soldiers jumped into the boat and searched it very carefully, finding nothing. Emily watched with satisfaction as they walked along the dock and only looked out into the weeds and grass.

The squad of soldiers searched the Thatchers' property for over an hour without finding a trace of their quarry. They left carrying nothing but the two smoked hams, which Mr. Thatcher gladly sacrificed.

After dark Mr. Thatcher went down to his dock, pried up the decking and led the lieutenant back up to the house where his wife and daughter were waiting. The young man looked at the father with deep respect. "I heard what the Yankee said to you down on the dock. What you did for me, what all of you did for me was brave almost beyond belief. I shall tell my friend about you, in case something happens to me. Some way I will make arrangements to repay your kindness."

Embarrassed by the emotion the young man expressed in this little speech, Mr. Thatcher said, "I'm sure your mother would have done no less for our sons. Now it's time for us to leave. I have made arrangements for some watermen to take you across Milford Haven to Gwynn's Island tonight. Tomorrow night, if the wind is right, others will sail you across the Chesapeake to the Eastern Shore." Mrs. Thatcher smiled and said, "I will pack a little food for you and wrap it in a bandanna." and she left the room. Mr. Thatcher left to hitch up the horses to the wagon. This left Emily and the young lieutenant alone together. Impulsively she took his hand, "Please take care and promise to come back to .....us." With a squeeze of her hand he said, "Emily, I will do my very best."

Shortly after, under clear skies and a full moon, the two men climbed up into a farm wagon and with a light snap of the reins started for the shore of Milford Haven. Once there, Mr. Thatcher introduced the lieutenant to the two watermen who were to take him across. There was no wind that night. The watermen muffled their oars and silently rowed across the body of water. It was a beautiful night. As the lieutenant looked up at a million stars on a black velvet blanket and the moon setting on the far horizon, he thought about the girl.

The winter passed, and as March 1865 approached, news of the war grew continually more disheartening. In the homes near Mobjack Bay food grew ever more scarce; farmers were eating their seed corn and Yankee patrol boats continually drove fishermen from the fishing grounds. Oil for lamps was no longer available, tea and coffee were a thing of the past, and wives took down their mothers' spinning wheels from attics and began spinning wool to make their own cloth. The Thatchers learned that their son Tom had been wounded, but would survive, minus an arm. The last they heard of their other son, Robert, was that he was still fighting with Lee.

On March 15th a horseman rode up to the Thatcher house and handed Mrs. Thatcher a letter. He rode off quickly without saying a word. The letter was from the young lieutenant. The family gathered together and Mrs. Thatcher read:

1 March 1865

Dearest friends,

My friend, whom I mentioned to you during my stay in your home, has made arrangements to get this unhappy missive to you. I have been captured by the Yankees. It happened two days before Christmas. My duties required me to deliver a message to a person in Washington who, unbeknownst to me, was already suspected by the Yankees as being sympathetic to our cause. I was seized at his door with the incriminating message on my person. So ends my career as a courier and spy.

From my cell window I can see the coming of spring. It will be early this year. I suspect the creek behind your home has been free of ice for some weeks now, and that the birds are already moving north. How I would like to have seen the Dogwood in bloom one more time. But it will not be. My guards say that they have delayed my execution too long already and that I am to be hanged in the morning.

Friends

Please do not mourn long for me. I knew the risk when I chose this path rather than one that would have me kill more mothers' sons. I have done too much of such killing. I thank you again for your kindness to me. Please pray for my soul.

John Richards, 1st Lt. CSA

Mr. Thatcher looked at his wife and daughter and said, "He was a fine young man. What a shame." Then they clasped hands, knelt, and prayed for John Richards, 1st Lt. CSA.

On the 12th of April the Thatchers received a second letter. This time Mr. Thatcher read the letter:

5 April 1865

Dear Mr and Mrs Thatcher and Emily,

I was a dear friend of John Richards. He spoke of you many times. I suspect that you are as devastated by his death as I am. I fear that our cause, that of the South, is lost. The blame for John's death and the demise of our way of life can be laid on the head of one man, Abraham Lincoln.

That man and others like him, and by others I mean Generals Sherman, Grant and Sheridan, are without honor. I cannot accept that my dearest friend had to die at the hands of such men. I will yet strike a blow for them and for the South! Sic Semper Tryannis![1]

Yours Truly,
John Wilkes Booth

1   This story is based in a general way on a legend told on the Middle Peninsula until the 1930s. In "Friends," Booth is the only familial name that is accurate. However, the legend and "Friends" are based on a real character, a Confederate spy by the name of John Beall. He was also a captain in the Virginia fleet of the Confederate navy. He was a schoolmate of Booth and he was hanged. According to the legend, Booth told Lincoln that if Beall were hung, he (the president) would die. Apparently there is no truth to this purported connection between Beall's hanging and Lincoln's assassination. "Having shot the President, Booth leaped down to the stage of Ford's Theater, crying out "Sic semper tryannis!"
See: *Virginia Folk Legends*, Edited by Thomas E. Barden, University of Virginia Press, Copyright 1991.

The Hero

The Hero

The young Confederate soldier had lost most of his blood and no longer felt much pain. He knew he was dying and could see the bodies of many of his comrades, also lying unmoving, in the cornfield about him.

Jed was eighteen years old and had been raised on Bayberry Creek, in Lancaster County, Virginia. The date was June 27th, 1862. The young soldier and his friends had been fighting near a place called Gaines Mill. The field where Jed lay was at the foot of a high hill, alongside a creek which emptied into the Chickahominy River. He had been dragged down the hill to this cornfield by his friends. The earthy smell of the field reminded him of the farm where he was born and of his family.

He remembered the love and worry in his mother's sad eyes when he marched off with his friends to the war. She had hugged him tightly and said, "Jed, be careful and come home as soon as you can. And remember, no matter what they tell you, every human life is precious." His mother did not hold with fighting of any kind. He smiled as he thought of her.

He no longer seemed able to move, but he could still feel the warmth of the late afternoon sun on his face just like it felt on the day he left home, three months ago. Jed had felt badly about leaving the spring farm work to his pa and younger brother, but the Northerners were trying to take away their rights and young men were needed to defend the Confederacy, or so the recruiter said. Pa was too old to join up and his brother, Jeremy, was only fifteen years old. Jed figured if they were going to fight, he had better go and help them before the Yanks carried the war to Lancaster County. Besides, Jed had won the last turkey shoot contest and all his friends knew that he was very good with a musket.

Once Jed joined his company, the Lancaster Grays of the Fortieth Virginia Infantry, he learned that if there was one thing soldiers respected besides bravery, it was marksmanship. His comrades and officers quickly realized that he was the best shot in the company. They also knew that he had acquired this skill by hunting and his sergeant often gave him a pass and sent him off alone to see if he could shoot fresh meat for the cooking pot.

By the first of June, Jed had been with the Grays for eight weeks, but he still had not seen any military action. He listened to his many friends talk about earlier combat. Like most young soldiers he worried about how he would react in battle. His friends gave him lots of advice, but two remarks seemed to make the most sense. The first one came from his sergeant, who said, "When the fighting begins, just stay with your squad and do what I say." The second remark came from a private who had been in several battles. He said, "When the shooting starts, ignore the bluecoat officers, shoot the privates, because they're the ones who will be trying to kill us. The way I figure, the fewer of them left, the better our chances of getting home."

A few weeks later, the Grays made camp in late afternoon, after an eight-hour march. The company was tired and hungry. The countryside through which they had tramped was mostly rolling farmland with an occasional wood lot and pond. Rain had fallen recently and in some of the nearby fields dark green winter wheat gently undulated as the soft summer breeze passed across it. In fields planted with corn, the young stalks were pressing up to a blue sky filled with popcorn clouds. To a farm boy, the day was one of promise. Jed never knew whether the sergeant asked him to go hunting that day because the company really needed meat or because he knew that he was homesick.

Early in the hunt Jed had shot a large wild turkey, but after that he had walked several miles without seeing anything. Finally, on the horizon, he saw a small copse of trees growing along what appeared to be a depression. He thought, *I'll bet there's a pond on the other side of those trees. Maybe I'll find some ducks there.* Jed walked briskly but still it took nearly ten minutes to reach the spot. As he looked down the sloping ground, he saw a pond glinting between some sweet gum trees. Bayberry bushes grew thickly between the trees and provided cover as he crept to the water's edge.

As Jed neared the pond, he heard a sound that started his heart pounding. Laughing! It was laughing! The sound seem to be coming from in the pond. He drew back the bayberry branches very carefully and looked out over the water. Two men were swimming near the opposite shore. They were naked. The pond was long and narrow and the far shore was bordered by a long sloping hill, a pasture which was devoid of protective cover. At the end of the pond, perhaps two hundreds yards away from the men, Jed saw two muskets propped against a tree, what appeared to be a pile of dead ducks, and two BLUE uniforms. *Yankees!* And they were PRIVATES!

Jed carefully eased the limbs of the bayberry back to their original position. He quietly placed the turkey he had been carrying on the ground. His palms were sweaty, his hands were shaking, and his breath came in gasps as if he had been running uphill. He forced himself to think. *They're sure to see me if I try to sneak around and capture them. But it's an easy shot from here. I could get one and probably the other before he could get to his gun.* The boy was on his belly now and he moved slightly to the right where the branches of the bayberry thinned out near the ground. The naked men were standing now, waist-deep in the water. He eased his weapon forward. There was a patch of dark hair in the center of the white chest of the nearest big private. *A perfect target,* he thought. He eased the hammer back on his musket and it locked in place with the loudest metallic "click" he had ever heard a weapon make. He stared at the men in disbelief. They hadn't heard the noise. They continued their horseplay unaware that death was about to strike one of them.

Jed was talking to himself under his breath. *Line up the dark patch in the sights, steady the gun, take a deep breath. Squeeze the trigger.* As his mind spoke the words, his body dutifully reacted to each command. His hands steadied as his finger began to pull on the trigger. But he hesitated when he heard a soft voice in the back of his mind say very clearly, "Every human life is precious." Jed responded. *He's a private, he'll kill me if he gets the chance.* But the voice only repeated softly, "Every human life is precious."

Jed lowered the hammer on his musket and quietly withdrew from the bushes. He almost forgot the turkey, but saw it at the last moment and dragged the bird away with him. He hurried back to the encampment and gave it to the sergeant. Before he could say anything, the sergeant thanked him and said that there were bluecoats in the vicinity and that they would be moving out early in the morning. Talk around the campfire was that General Lee was going to attack the Yankees soon. He had beaten them at every turn and was looking for a decisive battle.

That had been a week ago, and although his company had skirmished several times with the Yankees, Jed had not been in a single major battle. But that day they caught up with the retreating Yankees and he knew that the battle that he had anxiously anticipated and feared was about to begin.

Jed clearly remembered moving into a line of battle in some trees near the foot of the long sloping hill. He was scared. They all were. But there were THOUSANDS of men in butternut uniforms, surely enough to carry the hill. They waited for orders. They checked their weapons, and checked them again. They prayed. They waited some more. Jed was anxious now for the attack to begin because he had been told that if they gave the bluebellies one more good whipping the war would probably end and they could go home. He looked at the cannon pointed at them from the top of the hill they were about to charge. *Maybe the Yankee's line wouldn't break this time.* He prayed harder.

He saw puffs of smoke on the top of the hill and a fraction of a second later he heard a deafening roar. The cannons had begun firing. He remembered thinking, *it's not like thunder, there's a pause between thunder claps.* This noise was incessant, it hurt his ears, it made the contents of his stomach crawl toward his throat. Finally, the sergeant called to them to close ranks. They pressed together, shoulder to shoulder. The command came to move out and they started up the long slope. Within yards they were stepping over the bodies of their comrades who, only moments before, had gone before them. Some were dead, others moaned piteously as they clutched at their wounds or tried to drag themselves to safety. Jed and the men in the ranks kept on. Men, and parts of men, disappeared as cannon shells began ripping holes in their line, but they kept on. When the men in gray reached the half-way point, the cannons switched to grape shot. On Jed's right a dozen men were cut down en masse by the grape scythe. The rest pressed on. Soon individual men were being knocked to the ground by musket fire. Still the gray line moved forward.

At last, the call to charge. He remembered the Rebel yell screaming from hundreds of throats, over and over. He remembered trying to aim his musket, trying to run up that hill, seeing the BIG YANKEE PRIVATE aiming his musket at him, the searing pain and then the great quiet. Finally, he remembered regaining consciousness.

Looking up at the blue sky and smelling the cornfield, he remembered it all. But now, very clearly, he saw home; Ma, Pa and Jeremy, and with a deep sigh the young hero closed his eyes a final time.

Old Max

Old Max

They called him Old Max. Dan, his master, claimed he was a purebred black Labrador, but others said he also had a touch of Weimaraner or some such other friendly beast in his genetic makeup. He was neither old—he was born four years before the events of this story took place—nor entirely black, as tufts of grey fur grew in profusion about his shoulders, near his paws and along his tail. He was an outside dog. He loved the woods and the water, but most of all he loved to hunt ducks and birds and other small game.

Old Max worshipped his master and his master's friend, Jim, mainly because they were the ones who took him hunting. When Dan and Jim would call him over to the pickup truck with his cage in back, he knew that if either of the men carried a gun, there was going to be a hunt. And his instincts, bred of untold generations of hunting ancestors, would drive him nearly wild in anticipation. It was the same set of instincts that caused him to run far into the woods, to a secret place, to bury the bones that Dan and his wife gave him.

On a Thursday morning, the day that this story began, the two men called Max over to Jim's pickup truck. Jim was carrying a shotgun, but Max already knew from the way that they were scratching his ears, his rump and his chests and doing the other foolish things that men do, including repeating over and over "Ducks boy, ducks", that he was going hunting. He yipped, whined, and chased his tail a little—because he knew Dan and Jim liked to see him do that—and jumped up into his cage in the back of the pickup. Dan could not get off work that morning to go hunting, but he insisted that Jim take Old Max and go without him.

That Dan would let Jim take Old Max hunting was a measure of their friendship. Dan felt that Max was the best retriever in the county and maybe in the state. He had heard talk in the local bars that out-of-state dognappers were always on the lookout for dogs of Max's quality. He didn't know if he should believe the rumors but he didn't believe in taking chances either. Out of his owner's sight, a dog could be easily snatched, especially one as friendly as Old Max. So no one but Dan or Jim ever took Max hunting.

The friendship between Jim and Dan had begun forty years earlier, in high school, when they discovered their common love of hunting. Now, both men were in their sixties and had thinning hair and thickening waist lines. In addition to hunting, they were drinking and fishing buddies, they followed the same sports teams, attended the same church, and married girls who were best friends. Jim and Dan were far from well-to-do, but they lived comfortably with their wives on the banks of Bayberry Creek. Every Thursday evening, they played penny-ante poker with two of their other cronies.

After fastening the latch on Old Max's cage in the back of the pickup, Jim drove to one of his favorite hunting spots near the Corrotoman River. He had been hunting birds without success along the river bank for an hour or so when Max flushed a covey of doves. Jim swung his shotgun up and with two quick shots knocked down two birds. Max bounded into the underbrush and in seconds returned with a bird. The dog charged back into the brush and, in what seemed like no time at all, was back with the second bird. The two doves had fallen near the water's edge and to Jim's surprise the dog headed back toward the river a third time. He waited and although he called, Max did not return. As Jim approached the river he could hear Max growling.

He saw Max pulling at something in the sand just below the high tide line. It was not like the dog to be diverted from the hunt. Jim thought, *maybe he's found something dead. Jeez, I hope he doesn't roll in the stinking stuff.* But what Max had found was not the remains of an animal. As Jim watched, the dog pulled an old teapot from a rotting wooden box.

The teapot appeared to be pewter and Max gripped it firmly in his jaws by its black wooden handle. Jim couldn't tell what kind of wood the handle was made of, but it must have tasted good to Max because he was reluctant to give the pot to him.

Jim tickled Max's nose with the tail feather from one of the doves until the dog released the teapot and carried the pot back from the river's edge. He sat down with his back against the rough bark of a giant loblolly pine and examined the teapot carefully. It was shaped like a cylinder but was fluted vertically around its entire circumference. Its height was about the same as its diameter. The spout was fastened to the bottom of the pot and angled upward at forty-five degrees. The curved wooden handle was inserted into pipe-like protrusions at the bottom and top of the teapot. Jim rubbed the side of the teapot on the sleeve of his rough woolen shirt. It shone. The pot looked like it was made of silver, not pewter! He searched the base carefully for a hallmark or the maker's initials. He saw what appeared to be slight indentations on the underside, and when he rubbed it with his sleeve the initials *P.R.* appeared along with the number *17*. He rubbed the spot harder and saw *P.R. 1775*. Jim was never very interested in history when he was in school, but he had a good memory. As soon as he saw the initials and the number, a poem from his school days came to mind.

> *Listen my children and you shall hear*
> *Of the midnight ride of Paul Revere*
> *On the eighteenth of April, in Seventy-five*
> *......"*

And then he said aloud, "Naw, it couldn't be." But then he thought, *but the year is right, and Paul Revere was a silversmith. Maybe it could be.*

Jim stood up and headed back to his pickup truck. Old Max sensed the hunt was ended and hung back. The sun was still rising. It was only mid-morning. They could hunt for hours yet. Why did this dumb man want to stop? The man opened the door to the dog cage in the bed of the pickup truck and called, "Max, come." The dog slowly walked to the truck with his head down and his tail between his legs. He refused to look at Jim even when he felt him scratching the spot where his tail joined his body.

Max knew that he would not be flushing any more birds this day, nor smelling any more of the wonderful odors that drifted in the air along the water's edge, nor even chasing an occasional squirrel or rabbit through the underbrush. Once he was in the cage, he lifted his leg and peed through the bottom grate onto the floor of the pickup. He knew the man hated that. Jim didn't curse him as he expected but jumped into the cab of the truck, started the engine, and raced off in the direction of the dog's home.

Fifteen minutes later, he pulled into Dan's drive, got out of the truck's cab, and let Old Max out of the cage. Without looking at the man, the dog leaped to the ground and left at a trot for the nearby woods. Dan lived in a rural area and most owners let their dogs roam freely about the neighborhood, so Jim let him go. He jumped back into his truck and headed home to show his wife the teapot.

If anything, Jim's wife, Nell, was more excited by his find than he was. She cleaned and polished the pot until it shone like new. That afternoon she phoned authorities at various Virginia universities and at the Smithsonian Institution in Washington, D.C. and described the teapot to them. They all said the same thing. "It looks like your husband may have found an authentic Revere piece or an excellent imitation." When she asked the Smithsonian expert if it was valuable, he said, "Very, very, valuable."

Nell was delighted. She put the teapot in a place of honor in their foyer, just inside the entrance to their house. It sat on a lace doily, in front of the cherished antique mirror which had been given to her by her grandmother. Then she started phoning all of her friends.

That evening Jim went to Dan's house for the usual Thursday night poker game. Dan and Jim had been playing poker together for many years. It was a friendly game, usually with four players. The two men, with signals known only to them, often would help each other to build up the pot when one of the two had a particularly good hand. The cheating was harmless since the pots never amounted to more than ten or fifteen cents and they never were really assured of winning. At the end of the night, after the other two men had left, Jim and Dan would toss their winnings, if any, into a gallon jar. They had started this little ritual in the early sixties, over thirty years ago. It was their intent to use the contents to take a goose-hunting trip to the Eastern Shore of Maryland. The gallon jar was nearly full. They stored it in a closet with several other full jars.

On this night, within a few minutes of sitting down at the table, Jim told his poker buddies about shooting the doves and finding the teapot. Dan was only moderately interested in the tale until Jim mentioned Nell's conversation with the Smithsonian expert. Then his eyebrows shot upward. "Jim, did you say that the expert said the teapot was very valuable?"

Jim guessed what Dan was thinking. "Yes, that's what he said. But don't worry. If we sell it, I'm going to give you a share of the money." Dan's face wore an expression that Jim had not seen before. "You're not going to give me a share Jim, you're going to give me the teapot, 'cause it was my dog that found it."

The argument that followed involved not only Dan and Jim, but the other two card players as well. One of them sided with Jim and the other with Dan. Outside in his doghouse Old Max heard the racket and it confused him. He had never heard Dan and Jim raise their voices in anger to each other before. His discomfort further increased when Dan's wife, Alice, returned a few minutes later. As her car pulled into the driveway, Jim came storming out of the house. The two people glared at each other as they passed on the sidewalk. The dog sniffed the air, barked and looked into the eyes of the man and the woman as they turned to look at him. They were both very angry, he could see it in their eyes and even at a distance, he could smell it.

Alice and Nell, and several of their friends had started their own gin rummy party several years earlier so that they would not have to spend the evening alone when their husbands played poker. On this particular night, the party had been at Nell's house. Nell told the story of the teapot, with emphasis on its value. Alice's reaction was the same as her husband's. All the ladies present took sides in the argument and like the poker party, the gin rummy party broke up early.

By the next day everyone who lived in the nearby town of Kilmarnock had heard the story of the teapot and all the citizens took sides in the dispute. The minister of the church, that the feuding families attended, tried to solve the matter by suggesting that the teapot be donated to the church. The proposal was almost accepted, then someone asked indelicately, "Who is to get credit for the donation?"

Three weeks later the argument still raged. Dan threatened to sue for the teapot and hired a lawyer. Jim threatened a counter suit on harassment grounds and he hired a lawyer too. Another week passed.

Old Max was miserable and totally confused. The season was moving on and he had not been on a hunt since the last full moon. He moped about the yard and made frequent trips out to his bone graveyard in the woods where he would dig up a choice knuckle and, in an elemental way, contemplate his predicament. He thought about the last hunt. What had he done that had so angered his friends that they would not take him hunting again?

The following week events came to a head. The two lawyers met and decided that they would get the aggrieved parties together in one place and arbitrate an out-of-court solution. It was a beautiful Indian summer day. The pine trees were dropping cones by the thousands; the dogwoods, gums, oaks and maples had begun to cover the forest floor in a carpet of red and gold; and all the small creatures of the woods, swamps and farm fields were cavorting about enjoying the last warm days before the cycle of freeze-thaw-freeze began along the great rivers of Virginia's Northern Neck. In a dog's world, a perfect day for hunting.

Dan and Jim, their wives and the two lawyers, all of whom knew one another, met on neutral ground; they sat at a picnic table under an oak tree overlooking Bayberry Creek. The first question was posed by Dan's lawyer. "Where is the object in dispute?" Jim's wife responded testily. "Where it belongs. On the table in the foyer at our house." Dan's lawyer, looking just a little annoyed responded, "We need to have it here." The place where they were meeting was only a few minutes walk from either of the two families' houses. Nell, a bit ashamed of her outburst, said, "I'll go get it," and immediately set off on foot for her house.

A few minutes later they saw her returning. She was hurrying along at a half run. Her face was very white. Her hands were empty. As she approached, Jim called, "What's wrong? Where's the teapot?" Nell was perspiring. She was trying to straighten her dress, which she had hiked up above her knees so that she could run, and at the same time she was trying to tuck up several strands of hair which had fallen down over her left eye from the bun at the top of her head. She gasped, "It's gone, stolen!"   As one, Jim and Dan, the two lawyers, and Alice were on their feet and running for Jim's house. As they approached the front porch they could see that half of the screen on the door was pushed in. Reaching for the handle, Dan said "It looks like someone kicked it in. Let's notify the sheriff."

The sheriff arrived shortly thereafter. He said that it looked like someone had looked in the door, seen the silver teapot, kicked in the screen, grabbed the teapot and ran. Then he frowned, "This sort of thing is very rare around here, doubt if we'll ever catch the perpetrator. Bye folks."

The two lawyers looked at their respective clients. Then simultaneously they reached into their briefcases and pulled out slips of paper. Dan's lawyer spoke first. "Here's my bill, $325." Dan's mouth opened but he said nothing. Jim's lawyer spoke up, "My bill is only $250, because I didn't work on the case as long as he did."

At this point, Dan found his voice.

"I don't have that kind of money."

"Neither do I," said Jim. "Well, you have thirty days to pay," said the first lawyer. "Right," said the second lawyer. Dan looked at Jim. "What are we going to do now?" Jim thought a minute and smiled. "There's always the poker money in the jars." Dan grimaced, "But I owe more money than you do." Jim nodded, "Yeah, but what's a few bucks among hunting buddies, especially when the poorer one has a great dog?" Dan's right hand reached for his friend's.

The lawyers left and Nell looked at her husband and his friend and his friend's wife. "I've got a big ham in the oven. Why don't you all stay for dinner." And they did.

Later that evening Max saw Dan and Jim put his cage in the back of the pickup and place their shotguns in the rack behind the seat. He heard Dan say, "Let's try to get out in the fields by first light in the morning. We ought to have good hunting." Max didn't understand much of Dan's talk, but he understood the word "hunting."

Nell came out shortly after this exchange and gave Max a big ham bone. He savored it for a moment and then trotted off to his bone graveyard in the woods. Once there he looked around. Over the last couple of years he had buried so many bones that there were very few unused spaces left. He went to a spot he had used earlier in the day. Maybe he could make room next to the teapot.

The Otter

The Otter

The winter had been brutal on the Northern Neck. Despite the rise and fall of the tide, in the morning the larger rivers had slush ice on them and the creeks, more often than not, were frozen over. At 6 A.M. John shined his flashlight on the thermometer tacked to the wall outside the garage door, and saw that it was ten degrees, but did not mind the cold. He wore woolen underwear, a woolen shirt, a woolen sweater and a hooded Virginia Tech sweatshirt. He also wore a woolen navy watch cap, earmuffs, and heavily insulated rubber boots. He had been tramping through woods and swamps near his home for two hours and, except for his hands, the exertion had kept him warm.

He opened the small garage door, stepped inside, walked to the center of the room and dropped a burlap bag to the floor. It hit the cement with a dull thud. He pointed his flashlight upward, and with the beam found the pull-string to the light bulb that hung from the ceiling. With a tug on the string, he turned on the light. The sun would not rise for another thirty minutes and he needed the light of the bare 200 watt bulb for his task. He lit an old heater standing in the corner of the room. For a few minutes, before the flame burned hotly, the foul smell of kerosene assailed his nose. He opened the window a crack. Then, he went to work.

Standing on a chair, he ran a heavy cord through an eye bolt in a rafter which supported the garage roof. He opened the burlap bag and took out one of three dead muskrats that lay inside. He tied the cord tightly around the tail of the muskrat and adjusted it so that the animal hung chest-high in front of him. He removed his skinning knife from its sheath, picked up an Arkansas stone that lay on a nearby bench, and honed the blade until it was razor sharp. Then he began the skinning process.

Deftly he ran the knife around the base of the tail at the point where the leathery appendage met the soft undercoat of fur, then made the same kind of incision around each foot. Moving back to the hind legs he ran the point of the thin blade under the hide, cutting it from the circular incision at the foot to the circular incision at the base of the tail. He repeated the operation on the other leg. Grasping the fur near the tail, he pulled it from the carcass toward the head. As he pulled, he trimmed away fat from the hide. When he was finished the pelt was inside out and resembled a small wet leather bag. He slipped the bag over an expandable metal frame and by adjusting the frame, stretched the hide until it was as taut as a drum. Then he scraped off the remaining fat. Little or no blood resulted from the skinning process, but still he disliked this aspect of trapping. He skinned the two remaining muskrats in the same way. When he was finished he cleaned up the garage and headed for the house to get ready for school.

As he entered the house his mother called to him, "John, take your boots off in the utility room and clean up in the wash tub." She told him this every morning as he came in from his trapline. He thought, *I'm seventeen, fully grown and Mom treats me like Kevin.* Kevin was his twelve-year-old brother. John was physically mature for his age. He was only of average height, but well-built and tough. He excelled in all kinds of sports and loved the outdoors. A pretty sophomore at his high school and his love of sports were the two things that got John involved in trapping.

The girl's name was Susan and it took John from the start of the school year until November to get up enough courage to ask her for a date. As it turned out, Susan was as anxious to go out with John as he was with her. After only two dates John asked Susan to go to the Valentine's Ball, a dance second in importance only to the prom. She accepted, of course. At the time, the dance was several months off, but it was semi-formal and expensive. John's finances were dismal. He played football in the fall, basketball all winter, and baseball in the spring. In the summer, he worked on neighboring farms, but during the school year he did not take any part-time job that might interfere with his sports. His dad, who was also an avid hunter and fisherman came up with the answer—trapping.

Trapping appealed to John only because he could set his traps in the late evening and check them in the early morning. The muskrats fed mainly after dark. If he had an out-of-town game or would be gone for any reason, he simply removed the bait or left the traps unbaited. John's home was on a plot of land midway between two creeks, called Little Mill Creek and Big Mill Creek. His trapline took him from his home to the marshes at the headwaters of Little Mill, down the creek to where it emptied into the Corrotoman River, along the river to the entrance of Big Mill Creek, up this creek to the marshes at its headwaters and from there back home. It was a circuit of about four miles.

As he sat on a stool pulling off his boots, John was concerned about the results of the week's trapping. He had caught three rats in the large marsh at the headwaters of Big Mill Creek last night and six others there in the preceding six nights, but nothing at all in Little Mill Creek. Yet, the week before last, he had seen all kinds of signs of their presence.

John thought, *With the cost of traps and bait if I don't catch at least twelve to fifteen rats a week, I won't have enough money for the dance.* It was Friday and this weekend would be a bye weekend for basketball, meaning there would be no game. John thought, *Tomorrow I'll go back to Little Mill during the day and see if I can find the problem.*

After lunch the following day, John went into the utility room, pulled on his insulated boots and put on a single sweater and his down vest. After seven days of below freezing temperatures, the sun was shining brightly as he left the house. He checked the thermometer at the garage door. It read thirty-eight degrees. There was so little wind that even the dried leaves hanging on the oak trees in their yard were still. Soon John was walking briskly along the edge of a field where corn had grown last summer. The air was fresh and the blue sky was filled with small puffy clouds which reminded him of popcorn. The farmer who owned the field had run a disk harrow over it in the fall to prepare it for spring planting. The disked soil had thawed at the surface but was frozen underneath. Breathing deeply, John looked up at the sky and felt so good that he would have run, had his boots not been caked with mud.

Within minutes he entered the woods. The trees here grew in a series of deep ravines that trapped and guided rain and melting snow into the marsh and swamp that made up the headwaters of Mill Creek. The oak, beech and sweet gum trees were enormous. When the area was logged in the 1920s and 1930s, some sixty to seventy years earlier, the terrain was so rugged that the loggers avoided it. The ravines, and hills in between, abounded with wildlife. John walked quietly among the trees with a feeling of reverence. During the day he would usually see squirrels scampering about on the forest floor among a myriad of ground-feeding birds. If he didn't see them, he would stop and search high among the trees for the red-shoulder hawk, for whom the forest floor must have been a smorgasbord. Once he had seen one flash down, a streak of brown and white, and end the life of a sparrow in a puff of feathers as the luckless little bird had tried to feed among the fallen leaves.

John moved as quietly as he could down a ravine to where the ground became boggy and the marsh began. At this point the marsh was about 200 yards across. A half-dozen muskrat lodges were located thirty to forty yards out in the rushes. The lodges looked like sloppily-piled mounds of reeds and rushes. Normally they sat in patches of open water, but for the past week most of the marsh had been frozen over. When the temperature was near or just above freezing, like on this afternoon, the tide would open a narrow ribbon of water in the very center of the marsh.

John had been standing about fifteen yards from the edge of the swamp, partially hidden by some bayberry bushes, when he heard a chattering sound. He looked out over the marsh to the ribbon of open water. As he watched, a small brownish-black head popped up and made a chattering call. Almost immediately, John heard a response. Looking down the creek he saw a second animal's head sticking up from the water. Both animals dove, hardly making a ripple on the water. John thought, *My God, they're graceful.*

The air was very still and sounds traveled clearly across the ice and water. The next time he heard the chattering sound, he saw that the two animals were much closer together. The bigger of the two had a small fish in its mouth. The fish couldn't have been more than three or four inches long. He saw the animal take the fish in its paws and then with two swift bites it disappeared. John thought he could hear the animal's sharp teeth crunch as it bit through the little fish. *Otters*, he thought. *There are otters in this creek. The bigger one must be the male.*

The two animals surfaced one more time, chattered, approached one another very closely, then simultaneously dove under the water.

108

John watched the otters for another twenty minutes as they fished and talked to one another, then he walked out onto the ice to check the muskrat lodge. As soon as he moved, the otters saw him and dove. He did not see them again.

John moved around the muskrat lodges checking the underwater runways that the muskrats followed below the ice. The water was so shallow that when they traveled to and from their lodges their bellies cut grooves (runways) in the soft mud of the bottom. Around some of the lodges the grooves had collapsed, as if they were no longer in use. After looking around the marsh for any other signs that the muskrats had been active the previous night and finding little, John checked and rebaited his traps. He had caught nothing at Little Mill Creek. He continued down his trapline to the Corrotoman River and over to Big Mill Creek marsh where he found three muskrats in his traps. From Big Mill Creek, he returned home. He needed to have a talk with his father.

After dinner that evening he told his dad about his inability to catch any muskrats at Little Mill Creek. When he told him about sighting the otters, his dad frowned. "It doesn't surprise me that you're not catching any muskrats there. Otters are members of the weasel family, like mink. And like mink, they'll get into a colony of muskrats and kill them all. Otters are considerably larger than muskrats. If there are any muskrats left in the Little Mill Creek marsh it's probably because with all the ice and the low tides this week, the otters haven't been able to squeeze down the muskrat runways into their lodges. Oh, by the way, their pelts are worth twenty times more than the muskrats. But they are smart, like mink, and very difficult to catch. And they're travelers. Eventually they'll get over to Big Mill Creek." His dad's remarks were depressing.

John thought a minute and said, "Dad, they sure were fun to watch. They acted like they were talking to one another. Do you think that some animals can think or feel the way we do? Maybe just a little?" His father laughed, but then he saw that John was serious. "Well John, I really don't think so, but I've seen otter do things that make you wonder. Like the chattering you heard. That has to be a form of communication. And they play. They make mud slides on the river banks and use them to slide into the water over and over, so you know they're playing. I've even heard old timers say that otters throw stones into the river and dive in and try to catch them before they hit the bottom. But are they thinking or do they have emotions? I don't think so, but to be honest, I don't know for sure. But one thing I do know, they're getting your muskrats."

John had a date that evening with Susan. They went to Kilmarnock and rented a movie at the video store. They took it to Susan's house and watched it on her parents' big-screen television. It was a romance, *Sleepless in Seattle*. Susan thought it was great. John liked the score, although it was nothing more than a lot of old-fashioned music. He probably would have enjoyed the movie more if he hadn't been so distracted thinking about the otters.

Susan's folks were out for the evening and after a little mild necking, their conversation drifted around, as it often did, to the upcoming Valentine's Ball. They had volunteered to be on the decorating committee and Susan had all sorts of ideas involving red and white crepe paper, red tinfoil hearts and artificial flowers. As John listened to her excited talk and admired her blues eyes, her delicate features and the soft curves of her cashmere sweater, he thought. *She's the prettiest thing I've ever seen. I'm taking her to the Valentine's Ball, and if I want her to stay my girl, I'm really going to have to impress her.*

The following evening, Sunday, John took a bag of apples for bait and walked down to Little Mill Creek marsh. Dropping his bag of bait on the shore, he walked directly to the only muskrat lodge where he had seen signs of activity the previous day. The weather had once again turned very cold and the ice was solid under his feet. He followed a muskrat runway, which he could see clearly underneath the ice, from the muskrat lodge out to a point where the bottom began to drop off.

Using his hatchet, he chopped two holes through the ice. One hole was directly in front of the start of the muskrat runway. The other was about a foot to the left. Pulling up his sleeves, he reached down into the water and placed a trap directly on the bottom in front of the groove, in water too deep for a swimming muskrat to be caught, but shallow enough to catch an otter. A chain was fastened to the end of the steel trap. He took the chain in his right hand and reached again into the icy water. He passed the end of the chain under the ice to his left hand which he had thrust down the second hole, then drew the end of the chain out of the hole. It had a large ring at the end. He ran a long pointed stake through the ring and then drove the point of the stake deeply into the mud. He set no other traps in Little Mill Creek that night.

The following morning, John got up earlier than usual. He was that anxious to get down to Little Mill Creek marsh. He got dressed, put on his boots and ran to the marsh, falling twice enroute. As he approached the marsh he heard a noise.

He stopped in the trees a few yards from the marsh and looked out to the open water near the center. He saw the head of an otter lift out of the water and chatter, calling for its mate. It was the male and it seemed confused. He dove, swan twenty or thirty yards underwater, surfaced and called again. There was no answering call. The otter dove again, swam perhaps a hundred yards in the opposite direction, surfaced and called again. John sensed that there would be no answering call. He stepped out onto the ice. The otter immediately disappeared.

John walked out to where he had placed the otter trap. He could see the small dark lifeless form beneath the ice. It was the female. He chopped a hole in the ice and pulled her through. Caught by the trap, unable to surface because of the ice, she had drowned. John placed the otter in his tote bag and walked down Little Mill Creek toward the river to check his other traps on Big Mill Creek.

As he walked around the corner of the creek and out of sight of the marsh, he heard the plaintive call of the otter in the still morning air once again. *I won't tell Susan, how I earned the money*, he thought.

Redemption

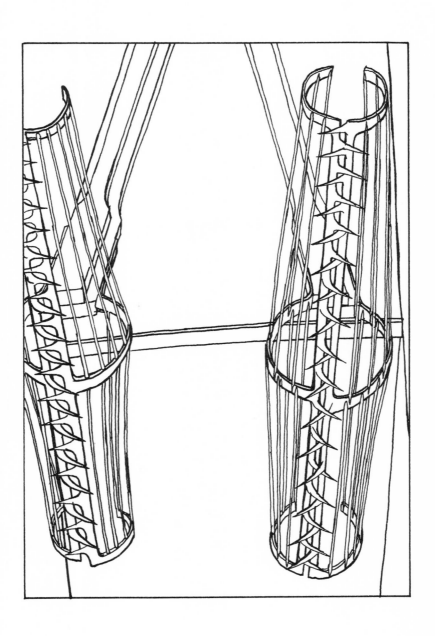

Redemption

Dave Haynard knew that he was waking up and he fought desperately against it. The memory of what he had done was returning, and waves of remorse began to envelop him. It was as if he had fallen into the dark waters of the Chesapeake Bay on a moonless night with a crab pot fouled about his leg. As he struggled, it dragged him down into its black depths. He tried not to think about what he had done, but even after all these years, it was indelibly imprinted in his memory. At work or rest it often drowned out all other thought. He lay back and silently wept.

He remembered his actions on that November day in 1940 as if they had happened only hours ago. He was young then and healthy. He knew that he was the best waterman on Bayberry Creek. He was thirty-two years old and had tonged oysters around the Chesapeake since boyhood, as his father and grandfather before him had done. But since the beginning of the season a new man was bringing nearly as many bushels of oysters to the buy boat as he. Although Flexel started earlier in the day, Dave worked as many hours or more. At first Dave could not understand how the man could be lifting so many oysters from his small oyster grounds. He was hand tonging alone. Eventually he suspected thievery and his suspicions were confirmed.

As he approached the tonging grounds through the cold gray mist of that November morning, Dave had seen Tom Flexel motoring away from a point near the ends of their adjoining beds. It was near the area where Dave had been harvesting far fewer oysters than normal. Dave was furious. Everything seemed obvious to him. Tom had been poaching on the Haynard oyster beds. "When I'm through tonging today, I'll settle with him. He won't be stealing anyone else's oysters," he muttered. But he never got the opportunity to give Tom the beating that he had in mind.

They tonged for about two hours. In his anger, Dave hurled oysters from the culling table to the pile that grew too slowly on the deck of his boat, the *Ann Marie*. Flexel was the one responsible for the meagerness of that pile! As Dave was preparing to move the *Ann Marie* to a new location, he looked at Flexel. He was less than a hundred yards away. Then Flexel jerked upright as his boat took a sudden turn. Dave almost laughed as the man pitched overboard. He saw Flexel surface and his mouth open in a call for help, but he heard nothing over the idling noise of the *Ann Marie's* engine. Instinctively, Dave started toward his boat's wheel to go to the man's aid, but once again his anger got the better of him. He saw Flexel grasp for the boat as he slipped under the water a second time. Dave thought, *serves him right, the man's a thief*. Then he saw Flexel, with a kicking motion, momentarily force his shoulders above the water. The effort seem to drain all his strength and he sank back.

Suddenly, only Flexel's arm was above the water, still grasping for the boat. *He's getting what he deserves*, Dave thought. In a few seconds more he sank from sight and only a cap floated on the surface where he went under. Dave put the *Anne Marie's* engine in gear and headed his boat to shore to call the sheriff. Dave, the sheriff and a group of oystermen recovered Tom Flexel's body later that day.

All semblance of a normal life ended for Dave Haynard three days later, when they buried Tom Flexel. It was the first time he saw Evelyn Flexel and her two children. He was not a religious man and had not attended the burial service at the church. He did not know why he had gone to the cemetery that morning, but he had. He stood near the small family group as the minister prayed and said a few final words at the grave site. The boy and the girl stood with their arms wrapped about their mother, tears streaming down their faces.

The family was relatively new to this part of the Northern Neck and it was a workday. There were only a very few other people at the cemetery. Dave watched the woman carefully. She was small with dark hair and eyes that were streaked with red and darkly discolored underneath. *It looks like she's done nothing but cry these past three days. Still, under normal circumstances, she must be lovely*, he thought. He looked at the girl. *She's a miniature of her mother, must be about eight years old.* He looked at the boy. He had light brown hair and blue eyes. *He's about fourteen. Must favor his father.*

His eyes moved back to the mother. She had an attractive figure and he liked the way her long dark hair fell in waves about her face and throat. He could feel a smile coming to his face. Suddenly, a sharp involuntary sob from the little girl momentarily drowned out the softly murmured prayers of the minister. It startled him. Then slowly the feelings of guilt began. *What kind of human being allows another man to drown, and then is physically attracted to his wife before the first shovel of dirt is dropped on his casket?* Thankfully, moments later the grave site service ended.

Before leaving the cemetery, he extended his condolences to the widow. She thanked him for coming and tried to make small talk. She asked him how his business was doing. He said, "Not bad." Then she added, "Tom said that something has gotten into your oyster beds and is reducing your take. I'll pray that whatever it is clears up quickly." He thanked her and said to himself. *The man must have lied to his wife to explain his successful oystering and my failure.* But the nagging feeling had returned.

With great effort Dave forced the memories of that funeral many years ago from his mind and swung his legs from the bed onto the floor. The cold linoleum on his bare feet distracted him from his unhappy train of thought. In his long johns, he walked through the sparsely furnished house into the kitchen. Although he electrified the house in the early 1950s, he had seen no need at the time to replace the old wood stove that he used to cook his meals. He stuffed kindling along with some pages from the *Rappahannock Record* into the stove and lit it. He put some water in the old coffee pot and set it on the stove to boil. Ten minutes later he threw in a handful of coffee grounds. When a strong aroma of coffee rose from the pot, he cracked a raw egg and dropped it, shell and all, into the brew. A moment later he poured the clarified coffee into an old mug and sipped from the steaming cup as the memory of how he learned to prepare coffee that way came back.

Three weeks after the death of Tom Flexel, Dave had paid his widow a visit. The Flexel home was much like his own except neater and more comfortably furnished. Also, school books on the dining room table and caps and mittens strewn about indicated the presence of children. Dave sat at one end of the kitchen table, with the children sitting on either side, and watched the new widow prepare coffee. Later, Dave had commented on the clarity of the final brew and Evelyn explained that she used a raw egg to clarify it. After finishing their coffee, Dave explained the purpose of his visit. He said that although Evelyn could sublease her dead husband's oyster beds, he thought that he had a better proposal. Looking at Evelyn and her son, he said, "I could work your oyster beds along with mine for a share of the profits. I would give you seventy-five percent and keep twenty-five percent. Tom Jr. would help me, as his time after school allowed. It will mean a lot of hard work for him, but I would teach him to be a waterman. When he is older, he can take over the work on your beds by himself."

The widow looked at Dave with genuine surprise. "Mr. Haynard, your offer is truly generous. It will mean much more work for you with little profit. Why would...." Dave interrupted. "I want to do this because we are neighbors and neighbors help one another. I'm a bachelor and the additional time at work means little to me. Besides, although I did not know Tom well, I thought him to be a fine, decent man." The words were hardly out of his mouth when Dave thought, *now I'm both a liar and a murderer.*

Dave looked at Tom Jr.. The boy was very excited. He grabbed his mother's hand. "Say yes, mom. I can do it. I can do it. We need the money." Dave continued to look at the boy. He thought, *he must know what he's letting himself in for.* Seeing his willingness to do a man's work, he immediately liked the boy. Mrs. Flexel reached out and grasped a hand of each of her children. "Mr. Haynard, we thank you for your offer and we accept. Please call me Evelyn." Dave held out his hand and shook hers and then young Tom's. For the first time since he had met her, Evelyn smiled. *My God*, Dave thought, *she's beautiful!*

The coffee mug, which began to burn his hands, brought Dave back to the reality of his own kitchen. *Well*, he thought, *at least I taught the boy well.* He was proud of Tom Jr. The boy had left school when he was only sixteen to work full time on the water. By that age he was able to work his father's oyster beds by himself. Dave had taught him how to maintain his father's boat; carpentry, caulking, and engine overhaul. He could do it all. And when the oyster season ended, he worked the pound nets. Dave had taught him that too. With time the boy grew to manhood and, with Dave's advice, bought a small farm which he worked in addition to his oyster beds. Together with Dave, he looked after his mother and sister. Tom Jr. married in 1947 and eventually had two sons. His first son was named Tom after his father and grandfather, but his second was named Dave.

The smell of smoke caught Dave's attention and he got up from his kitchen table and adjusted the flue on the wood cook stove. He thought, *it's hard to believe how many years have passed since Tom Flexel died. I've lived with this love and this guilt for all that time. It ends today. Maybe she will forgive me, maybe she will hate me till my dying day, but I will tell her today. What will Tom Jr. and Annie think?* He thought of little Annie. Of course she wasn't little now. She was married too with three children. He remembered watching her grow up. He remembered how happy she had been at her engagement dinner and how upset she had been with him afterwards.

The year was 1952 and for several years Dave had joined Evelyn, Tom Jr. and Annie for Sunday dinner. The young people called him uncle Dave and it pleased him to be considered a part of the family. On that particular Sunday, Annie prepared the dinner. Afterward she and her beau, Jeff, had announced that they were engaged and were planning to be married the following spring. After Jeff had left for his home, Annie had asked Dave if she could talk to him alone, out on the porch. Dave loved the young woman as if she were his own daughter. He knew that his feelings for her were affected by her appearance, for she looked very much like her mother.

Annie asked him two questions. She said, "Uncle Dave, will you give me away at my wedding?" He answered that he would be very pleased to walk down the aisle with her. As he watched the young woman, she took a deep breath and blurted out. "You love mamma don't you? I can tell by the way that you look at her. Why don't you ask her to marry you?" The question had caught Dave totally by surprise and he was at a loss for words. What could he say to her? He had allowed her father to drown, coveted her mother, molded her father's son in his own image, and agreed to walk down the wedding aisle with her in her father's place. Was ever a greater hypocrite born than he? Finally, he had mumbled something to Annie about not being free to marry and rushed back into the house. Annie was visibly shaken and angry and she never raised the subject again. He never knew whether she mentioned the conversation to her mother and he was afraid to ask.

119

The lid rattling on the coffee pot—he had forgotten to take it off the stove—roused Dave once more from his thoughts. It was not Sunday, but Dave donned his white shirt and only suit. This was the most important day of his life. He hoped for forgiveness, and although he was not a praying man, on this day he prayed for more than that.

Dave was so deep in thought that he found himself in front of Evelyn's house with no recollection of how he had gotten there. It was a cool fall day and as he reached up to knock on her door, he shivered. *It's not that cold*, he thought, but then he realized that, under his suit coat, perspiration had soaked through his shirt. He knocked and immediately he heard soft footsteps approaching. The desire to flee was nearly overwhelming and he almost lost his nerve. But then Evelyn was standing in the doorway.

She looked alarmed. "Dave, are you ill? You look terrible." As she led him into the kitchen, he said, "I must talk to you." She nodded. "All right, talk." He looked at her and started the story of what he had done to her husband that horrible day thirty years ago. He had no sooner started than he realized he would not be able to bear the look in her eyes when she heard his story, so he closed his own eyes tightly and plunged on. In a few moments he was done. She made no sound. In agony, he forced himself to open his eyes and look at her. She was weeping silently.

She looked at him with an expression he could not understand. She said, "Dave have you loved me all these years?" Looking down at his calloused and wrinkled hands, he said, "Yes, from the first day I saw you." She gave an agonized moan. "God, what have I done." She spoke in a rush. "Dave, Tom died from a massive heart attack, not drowning. The coroner was a friend and never told the sheriff. He knew how badly off we were financially and Tom's insurance paid double for accidental death." Then she sobbed, "I have loved you for these many years as well."

They stood and Dave did what he had wanted to do for thirty years. He took Evelyn Flexel in his arms.

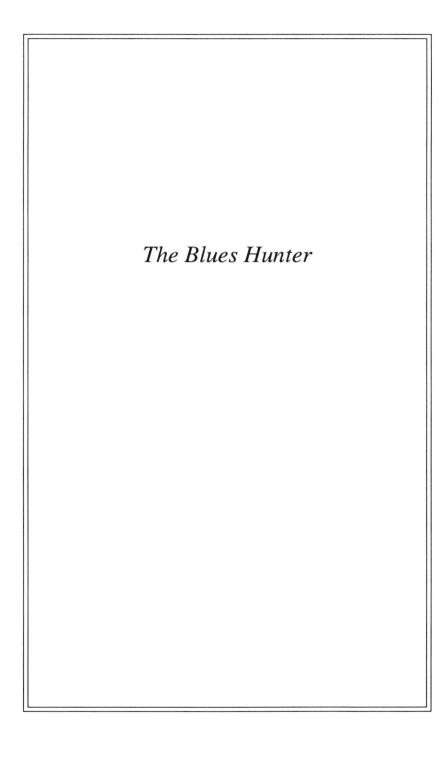

The Blues Hunter

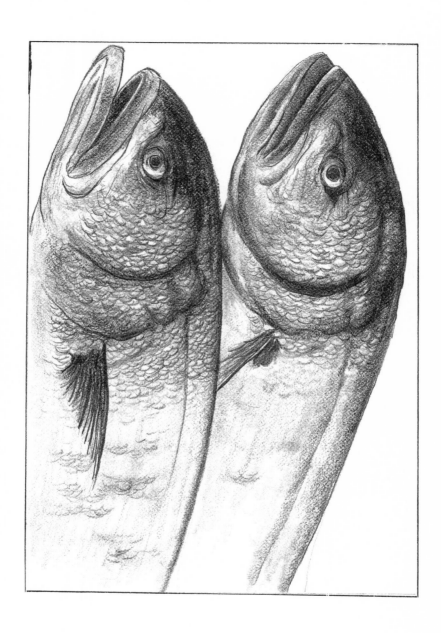

The Blues Hunter

It was mid-August and the drive from Washington, D.C. to Reedville, on the Chesapeake Bay, had taken nearly three hours. Even with all the windows open, the stifling heat in the old car made the couples' clothes stick to the vinyl seats and did nothing to improve the disposition of the driver. As they approached the lovely brick home on the Great Wicomico River Julie turned in the passenger seat and said to her husband. "Jack, please don't start arguing with your dad as soon as we're in the front door."

"Julie, I don't start the arguments, he does."

They had been married for three years and Julie kept expecting that the strained relationship between her husband and his father, Bud, would straighten itself out. At times, when his mother Janey, got the two talking about some happy event from earlier years, it seemed they were about to reconcile. But then one of the two men would sense what was happening and would make a remark that would set the other off.

The trouble began years earlier when Jack started college. His father was an engineer and owned a construction company which specialized in building bridges. He was very proud of the business and assumed that Jack would study engineering and come into the firm with him. Jack on the other hand wanted to be an artist and entered the fine arts department of a state college. His father could neither understand nor accept this. Everyone (especially engineers) knew about starving artists. How would Jack support himself, to say nothing of a family, after he graduated?

As they pulled into the driveway of the lovely home, they could see the sparkling waters of the Wicomico and Bud's fishing boat in its slip. Julie said, "Please Jack, for me, try not to argue. Tell your dad about your successful showing in Georgetown and the prices your paintings are starting to demand. Maybe that will bring him around." Jack laughed, "Not a chance hon, he'll never be happy until he sees a slide rule in my pocket, a transit in my hand, and mud on my shoes. The only thing dad and I have in common is our love of fishing. And even then, he's only happy when he catches a bigger fish than I do."

As they pulled up to the front door of the house, Jack's mother and father came out to meet them. Janey was beaming. But Bud looked at their car and frowned. "Old heap is still running, hey?" Jack ignored the remark, hastened up to his mother and gave her a hug.

After a quiet dinner, Jack and his father took their coffee out onto the deck and began to discuss the next day's fishing. Jack looked at his father's boat *The Blues Hunter*. She was an old wooden Chris Craft Sea Skiff on which he had built a flying bridge. Bud had also added several stainless steel-covered rub rails to her sides for protection as he took her in and out of his slip, which was more exposed to the wind than he liked. Her exterior was in Bristol condition and he took great pride in her appearance.

"I took her out this morning and found a large school of menhaden churning up the water about five miles southeast of Wicomico Light. I plan on leaving before first light in the morning and trolling from the Wicomico toward where I last saw the school. If we find it we'll switch to casting. The bluefish seem to be running large this year. I'd like to win this tournament just once in my lifetime. In twenty years I've only come close once."

Jack looked at his father. The man was seventy-two years old and, as far as Jack knew, he had only really wanted a very few things in his lifetime: To marry Janey, to have his own business, to have his son work with him in that business, and to win a major bluefish tournament. *Well*, Jack thought, *two out of four ain't bad. Jeez, what am I talking about! It ain't good!*

They left the following morning before first light. In the darkness, as Bud eased the *Blues Hunter* out of her slip, he bumped one of the pilings hard with his stern. But the only damage was to the end of the narrow stainless steel covering over a rub rail. It was bent out slightly. Keeping the flashing red markers to their left, they motored slowly down the Great Wicomico River toward the light that marked its entrance. As soon as they reached it they turned to starboard and took up a south-southeast course toward the point offshore where Bud had seen the menhaden the previous day. The sun was already halfway above the horizon, a glowing red mass, and the slight mist floating just above the surface of the water was rapidly dissipating. The water surface was unblemished by even the slightest breeze. The day was going to be a scorcher.

All around them other boats were beginning the day's fishing. Voices carried for great distances over the still water. Jack almost responded when he heard someone say, "How much chum we got?" Then other voices, "Get that beer iced down. . .Head west, more to the west. . .Let's go over to Smith Point lighthouse. . .Shiiit, if we go there, we'll have to fight our way through the boats."

After about twenty minutes they left the voices and most of the other boats behind. Bud slowed the boat to an idle. They got their boat rods out of their holders and snapped on their lures. Bud put the boat in gear and they began to troll. At 6:30 A.M., the temperature was in the low eighties already. They caught two small blues, too small to fool with, and threw them over the side. Then Jack thought he felt slight vibration through the soles of his shoes. At first he thought, *It's my imagination, its probably just a little water in the gas—condensation.* But it got worse! "Dad, when was the last time you tuned the engine?"

"Don't worry about it Jack, it always runs rough at low speed. Besides, we ought to be using the Merc anyway." With that he turned off the boat's Chrysler engine, walked to the transom and started the small Mercury outboard that he used for trolling.

But Jack was not satisfied with his father's answer. He opened the main engine box, took a socket wrench from a tool box and removed a spark plug. It was covered with black carbon. He took a small wire brush and a piece of sandpaper from the tool box and cleaned the plug. Then he removed and cleaned the other five. He said sarcastically, "I thought engineers were supposed to be good with engines." Bud said nothing. When Jack finished, he put the tools away and put the cover back on the engine box. And just in time. As he dogged down the last latch, the reel of his rod screamed and the pole bent nearly double in its holder.

Jack fought the fish for about ten minutes. He thought, *this is why I love fishing.* Bud netted the fish as Jack brought it alongside of the boat. "It's about ten pounds Jack, not a winner, but a nice fish." Jack looked down at his hands, still black with carbon from the plugs. "When was the last time you checked the plugs dad, they were a mess. They need to be replaced." It was not so much what he said but the way he said it. Bud snapped, "It's my boat, I'll take care of it the way I want. You should talk, your car's a mess." Over the next twenty minutes, they each caught two more fish. Each time Bud's was a little larger. He could not resist. "Guess the old man's still the better fisherman!"

For the next two hours they caught nothing and said practically nothing. They both knew the poor fishing was due to the slack tide. In spite of dark glasses, the sunlight reflecting off of the mirrored surface of the Bay made their heads ache. The temperature approached ninety-five degrees. Perspiration ran down their foreheads, stung their eyes, dripped off their noses and cascaded down inside their shirts. Even their kakhi pants were wet to mid-thigh.

At one point Jack almost said, "If the engine was running better, we could run into the marina until evening." But then he thought better. As he looked at his father fussing with his tackle in the shade of the tower, he turned and smiled, just a little. His hair was white and thinning slightly, but his dark eyes were still clear. He remembered how, when he was a boy, he could see the pride in those eyes whenever his father heard of his achievements. He remembered too the disappointment he saw in them when he told him that he was going to study art.

Bud was trying to untangle some lures. It would have been an easy task for Jack, but he could see that an involuntary shaking in his father's left hand made it difficult for him. When Bud finished untangling the lures, he grabbed one of the stainless steel pipes supporting the flying bridge and pulled himself erect, but he did not do it gracefully or easily. *My God*, Jack thought, *he's old, when did he get old?*

They had long ago reached the area where they thought they might find the school of menhaden, but the little fish eluded them. Now looking toward the eastern horizon Bud saw what appeared to be a large mixed flock of seagulls and terns near the surface of the water. Jack and Bud reeled in their trolling lines, killed the little Mercury, started the big Chrysler and headed for the birds and what they hoped was the menhaden school. Jack felt no vibration as the big engine

126

pushed them through the water at nearly thirty knots. While they headed for the birds, he attached lures to their spinning rods.

As they approached the birds they could see the school. Bud slowed the boat to near trolling speed and put the engine into neutral. They glided up near the edge of the school. The sea was a boiling mass of silver for several hundred yards, as if someone had dumped truckloads of Christmas tinsel into a raging current. Thousands of menhaden were swerving in unison, rising to the surface and diving, trying to escape the bluefish slashing up through the school from the depths. So vicious was the onslaught of the predators that parts of menhaden as well as whole fish could be seen in the swirling mass. Seagulls were screaming as they fought one another for the remnants, and the terns, true aerial hunters, simply dove and snatched one small menhaden after another.

Father and son looked at one another and smiled. And then they cast their lures as far as they could into the center of the swirling mess. They lost track of how many fish they caught and later they could not even make a good guess for as fast as they caught them, they threw them back. They were looking for size, not sheer numbers. Bud was thinking about changing lures when he hooked a fish that immediately went deep and bent his rod double. He adjusted the drag and played the fish. It ran for a hundred yards. He reeled it back fifty yards. The fish ran out another forty yards. After fifteen minutes of fighting, Bud was standing in a puddle of sweat. Jack wrapped the handle of his father's pole in an old rag to improve his grip. He watched as the fish and his father tired. It was going to be a close thing as to which gave out first. It took forty minutes, but they landed the blue. It weighed thirty-three pounds on Bud's portable scale.

They continued to fish the school, catching blues one after another. Both men were covered with fish blood and gore by this time. Although most of the fish were thrown back, some were too badly injured by the hooks to survive and they clubbed the snapping, struggling fish to death and threw them into a washtub. Then it was Jack's turn. The fish struck the lure once, twice, and then bit down and headed for the bottom of the Bay. A moment later it streaked upward, broke the surface and danced along on its tail, throwing its head back and forth trying to dislodge the hook. It dove again and then came near the surface in a last desperate struggle for survival. Jack heard his father yell, "It's bigger than mine! Bring it around to the side, where I can net it for you."

Jack had been fishing off the stern of the boat and as he fought to bring the fish to the port side of *Blues Hunter*, he caught sight of his father's fish out of the corner of his eye. *Mine is bigger*, he thought. Bud was shouting, "Keep the tip of your rod down, keep it down, or you'll lose him!" Looking down at the aft corner of the boat, Jack saw the bent stainless sticking out from the rub rail. With a single motion he dropped the tip of his rod down to the stainless, fouled his line, and with a sharp jerk upward severed the monofilament.

With a feigned look of dismay, he said to his father, "The damned fish dove under the propeller and cut the line." His father nodded and gave him a consoling pat on his shoulder.

Shortly after the loss of Jack's fish the menhaden disappeared into the depths. But it was late in the day and the two men were exhausted, so they headed for the shore and the tournament weigh-in station. At the official weigh-in Bud's fish tipped the scales at thirty-three and a quarter pounds, one and a half pounds less than the winner.

When the two men pulled into the slip, Janey and Julie were waiting for them. The men threw a washtub full of fish onto the dock and then walked up to the house, laughing and obviously reliving the day. All they said to the two women, after the obligatory kisses on the cheeks, was, "We'll clean the fish later." Bud put his arm around Jack's shoulder and shook him in a friendly way. "What a day! In the morning we'll change those spark plugs and try again." Jack smiled, "What a day!"

At bedtime, when she was alone with her husband, Janey said to him, "What happened?"

Bud gave his wife a bone-crushing hug and said "My son lost a prize-winning fish...for me."

Return from the Devil's Bottom

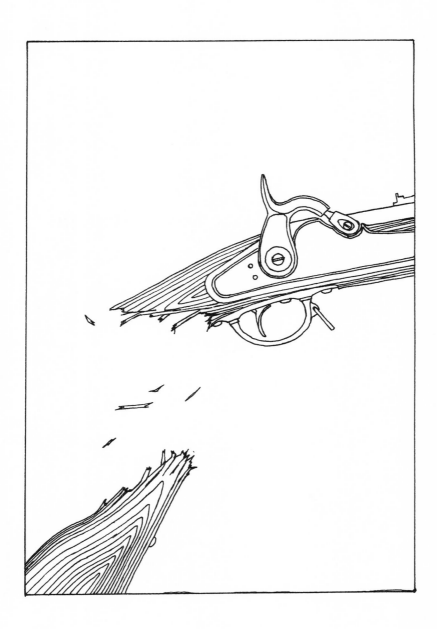

Return from the Devil's Bottom

Ewell had been waiting with his two companions in the ambush since shortly after sunrise. He sat with his back against a fallen pine, occasionally glancing over his shoulder in the direction that the Yankees would come. The ambush was set near the start of Bayberry Creek, in a depression called Devil's Bottom.

The canopy of a mixed forest blocked most of the sun's rays, but it was mid-summer and in the still air the heat was stifling. Beads of sweat ran down the boy's dark matted hair and trickled down the nape of his neck. The droplets felt like crawling bugs and every few minutes he would slap softly at them. Once, not more than fifteen feet away, he saw a small copperhead slither under a log that was half-covered by the decaying vegetation of the forest floor.

He cleaned his shoes with a stick and a handful of grass. He unloaded his musket. Cleaned it. Reloaded it. Counted the minie balls in his pouch. He ate some biscuits that he had stuffed into his pocket early that morning. It grew hotter. And still they did not come. He thought about his father.

It was July 14th, 1864, and Americans had been killing one another by the thousands for over three years. During the last week the Confederate general, Jubal Early, had fought his way through Maryland to the very edge of the nation's capital. His threatened attack on

Washington succeeded in drawing the Union's VI Corp away from the siege of Petersburg. Having accomplished this, Early recrossed the Potomac River at Leesburg, Virginia and began a strategic retreat down the Shenandoah Valley.

A bold land and sea assault, against the Yankee prison at Point Lookout at the mouth of the Potomac River, had been planned to coincide with Early's move against Washington. General Robert E. Lee had hoped his lieutenants would free thousands of his soldiers imprisoned there, but it had been called off at the last moment when the Yankees discovered the plan. Collaborators, who were to assist in the attack, had fled across the Potomac to the Northern Neck of Virginia, the peninsula situated between the Potomac and Rappahannock Rivers.

As these collaborators made their way toward Richmond and the Confederate lines, they advised their contacts in the Virginia Home Guard that the bluecoats would soon be on their trail. They also warned that the Yankees would probably try to confiscate livestock and foodstuffs.

Since all the able-bodied men of the Northern Neck were off fighting for the Confederate cause, the Home Guard was composed of old men and teenaged boys. Ewell and his friends, Jason, Jed and Charley were part of the Lancaster County Guard. After receiving the warning, his unit immediately fanned out across the county, advising people to hide their livestock and provisions. But this did not satisfy the four young men. They wanted to teach the Yankees a lesson. Since they knew the older members of the Guard would object, they planned the ambush in secret. The boys ranged in age from sixteen to eighteen. Ewell was the youngest.

This was not the first time that the bluecoats had sailed up Bayberry Creek from the Chesapeake Bay to forage. In the past, once they were well inland the soldiers would go ashore and collect grain, vegetables, and livestock for the war effort. It was this plundering that had goaded three of the young Virginians into setting the ambush. Ewell was motivated in a more personal way. His father had been killed fourteen months earlier at Chancellorsville.

When they received word of his death the boy had been overwhelmed with sorrow. For weeks memories of the man that he had loved so dearly filled his thoughts. Whether he was pitching hay, hitching up horses, planting corn or just doing his daily chores, he saw his father everywhere. At home the sadness in his mother's face reminded him of how his parents had loved and cared for each other.

In the evening, he remembered the long discussions the three of them used to have at the dinner table—and would never have again.

With time his mother slowly began to accept her loss, but Ewell remained unusually quiet and reticent. His mother knew how close he had been to his father and she thought that with time he would recover. He spoke little of his father's death and she did not know that it had left him with a consuming hatred for all men who wore the Union blue. Before his father left for the war he made Ewell promise to look after his mother and the farm. By regulations, he was still too young to enlist in the Fortieth Infantry, his father's Confederate unit, but he was big for his age and knew he could convince the recruiter to let him join up. On this hot July day, as sweat stung his eyes, he thought, *Pa, if only you hadn't made me promise.*

Ewell and his two friends were startled by the sound of feet running in the forest. A moment later the fourth member of their group, Jason, came around a curved bank of Bayberry Creek along a path into the bottom. He was panting and there was a wild look in his eyes. "They're coming! The bluecoats are coming! Four of them!" They took their positions behind the fallen tree. They lay about eight feet apart with the barrels of their muskets pointed out through some light brush that they had piled on the opposite side of the fallen tree.

Of the four men approaching the Devil's Bottom two were nearly middle-aged and two were young, not much older than some of the boys waiting in the ambush. The older Yankees were veterans. They had survived more than their share of battles. Both had been wounded and had recovered and counted themselves lucky to have been assigned to the Point Lookout Prison, for the assignment greatly improved their chances of returning to their families at the end of the war. The veterans also knew that there was little chance of overtaking the collaborators.

The four men walked one after the other around the curved bank at the end of Bayberry Creek and into the bottom. One of the veterans led the way. He was a big man and carried his heavy musket easily with one hand. The two young soldiers who followed him carried their muskets by the barrel with the stocks over their shoulders. The second veteran, a sergeant, walked at the end of the small column. He had known that it was going to be a hot day and had managed to exchange his heavy musket for a single-action Colt .44 revolver before the pursuit began.

In the ambush, Jed, the oldest of the boys, whispered, "Wait till they're all in sight." As the sergeant rounded the curve of the creek and stepped into the bottom Jed said in a loud voice, "Fire!" Four nervous boys jerked their triggers nearly simultaneously. Four muskets roared and acrid smoke filled the air.

The veteran leading the bluecoats was struck by three musket balls, two in the chest, one in the stomach. He died instantly. The young soldier next in line was struck in the side and fell to the ground screaming. The third soldier was pulled to the ground by the sergeant, who was already there. He had reacted instinctively at the roar of the boys' muskets. As he was going to ground, he pulled his Colt, cocked it and fired. And he kept on cocking and firing the Colt as he yelled at the young soldier he had dragged to ground. "Pull him behind the tree! Pull him behind the tree!" The meaning of his words finally dawned on the young soldier and grasping the legs of his wounded comrade he pulled him behind a large oak tree.

The Union sergeant's first shot went wild, as did the second. He knew the range was too great for his pistol, but he hoped his volley would slow the fire of the Rebels. His third shot missed. But despite the range the fourth struck home. The young trooper he had dragged to ground now was also returning fire. The Union soldiers had suffered dearly, but so had the boys. Their inexperience had betrayed them with the opening volley. The Union soldiers and the young Home Guards were not more than fifty yards apart, but instinctively three of Ewell's friends had aimed at the biggest and leading bluecoat. Ewell had wounded the soldier just behind the lead veteran.

When the shooting stopped, an elated Ewell yelled, "I got one!" and began reloading his gun. He was interrupted by a moan. Looking to his right, down the side of the fallen pine, he saw Jed on his back on the ground. There was a hole in his throat and the back of his head lay in a pool of blood and brain. *He was dead! The Yankees had killed Jed!* He heard the moan again. Looking beyond Jed, he saw that it came from Jason. He was sitting with his back against the pine. His right hand was pressed against his left shoulder. The hand, the shoulder and most of his chest were covered with blood.

He moaned again. Ewell crawled along the log to his wounded friend. When he saw the blood flowing from the hole high on the left side of Jason's chest, he choked and for a moment thought he was going to be sick. Jason had a bandanna tied around his forehead to keep the sweat from his eyes. Ewell forced himself to calm down. He pulled the wet rag from Jason's head, wrung the sweat out, folded it into a pad and pressed it against the wound. The bandanna was quickly saturated, but now the blood only oozed slowly from the wound. Jason looked at Ewell through eyes clouded with pain. "Ewell, who'll look after Mamma?" Jason's father was also serving with the Fortieth Infantry. Ewell squeezed his hand. "You're going to be all right Jason."

After patching Jason as best he could, Ewell looked over at Charley. Charley sat with his back tight against the tree and his knees drawn almost to his chest. He gripped the barrel of his musket with both hands. His knuckles were white. He had sat that way, without moving, while Ewell had worked on Jason. He stared at Ewell with a frightened look and motioned with his head in the direction of the Yankees. "We only got two of them, we only got two of them. I saw, we only got two. They're going to kill us."

"No they're not!" Ewell said with more conviction than he felt. "Reload, Reload. Load Jason's gun too. I'll load Jed's." After loading the guns, Charley looked at Ewell. "Let's get out of here." Ewell looked back at the way they had entered the bottom and realized that they were trapped. The only way out of the bottom was all uphill. They would be exposed to Yankee fire for a hundred yards. He looked at Charley and motioned with his head at the way out. "We can't, they'd shoot us before we got half way up the hill. Besides, we can't leave Jason. The Yanks can't leave either, except for the creek path they'd have to climb the hills too. If they try the creek path again they know we'll get them for sure."

After a while Jason began to moan softly again. Charley crawled over to Ewell. "Ewell, he's lost an awful lot of blood, if we don't get out of here soon, I think he's going to die." As if the Yankees were reading his thoughts, the words were hardly out of his mouth when a musket fired and a chunk of wood flew out of the log inches above his head.

In the excitement of the ambush, the boys hardly noticed the heat. But now it was past noon and the temperature was rising still higher. Jason was delirious. He called for water and then in an anguished voice, "Mamma, Mamma." Softly, a voice from the Yankee position seemed to respond, "Mamma, Mamma." Ewell was furious, "Only Yankees would be cruel enough to mock a wounded man."

But Charley grabbed his wrist, "No, listen." The voice floated softly across the forest floor from the Yankee position once again. "Mamma, Mamma." The agony in the voice was unmistakable. Charley looked at Ewell. "It's one of them Yankees we shot. He's dying too!"

Ewell took his water jug and crawled over to Jason. He pulled the cork, tipped the jug and let Jason drink. The water seemed to help. Jason's eyes cleared and he looked at Ewell. "They've killed me Ewell. Tell my. . ." He paused, out of breath.

Ewell put his mouth close to Jason's ear. "I'll get them for you Jason." But he could tell from Jason's eyes that he didn't understand what he had said. Ewell put his mouth closer to Jason's ear. "Jason, I'll make them pay, I promise."

Jason's eyes cleared once more and he said in a soft clear voice. "Tell my mother I'm sorry." Then he sighed deeply and died.

Jason had been his friend for as long as he could remember. Ewell thought, *Pa, now Jason. If the Yankees had known Pa and Jason, they never could have killed them.* He began to wonder what kind of men the Yankees were, but such thoughts were troubling and he focused instead on the immediate problem.

At the Yankee position, at almost the same time, a nearly identical death occurred. The sergeant lay the young soldier's head softly on his blue coat and said a prayer. Then he looked at the other young soldier who was now crouched behind a tree nearby and thought, *maybe I can save him.*

The sun seemed to reach its zenith and stay there. Time seemed not to pass at all. The boys lay drenched in sweat from their necks to their knees. They were filthy dirty and experiencing such fear that each boy, feeling his wet pants, thought that he had fouled himself. Every so often, they would crawl silently along the base of the log and nothing would happen. But if they made the slightest sound or movement that could be detected, a minie ball or a .44 caliber round would splinter the log just above them. Ewell thought that he must try something. Just beyond the fallen tree that they were using for protection was a second fallen pine. The rotting tree was somewhat smaller but still large enough to provide cover.

Ewell crawled over to Charley and told him his plan. He would crawl to his end of the fallen tree and using his musket and Jason's, fire two shots in quick succession to distract the Yankees. At his end of the tree, Charley would leapfrog to cover behind the next fallen tree when Ewell fired his second shot. If the Yankees didn't shoot at him, Charley could assume that he had made the move unseen. They would wait awhile and Ewell would draw the Yankees' fire again. But this time, with a much better angle of fire, Charley would whip his musket over his log and shoot one of the two exposed Yankees.

In a few minutes Ewell and Charley were in position at either end of their fallen tree. Charley signaled that he was ready. Ewell thrust his musket over the fallen tree and fired without exposing his head. The return fire was immediate but he hardly noticed. He scrambled about six feet toward the end of the tree farthest from Charley. He had left Jason's weapon there and he whipped it over the tree and fired. This time the return fire missed his head by a fraction of an inch. But when he looked, Charley was behind the next fallen tree. The Yankees hadn't seen him make his leap.

Less than four feet of open ground separated the two trees that shielded the boys. They crawled to the ends of the trees nearest this open ground and reviewed their plan again. They thought it might be a good idea to wait for at least a half hour before trying it. Maybe by then the Yankees wouldn't be quite so alert. Ewell hoped so, because this time he intended to aim his second shot and that meant his head and most of his shoulders were going to be above the fallen tree.

By nearly mid-afternoon Ewell and Charley gathered enough courage to go ahead with the plan. They moved to opposite ends of their logs so that Charley would have the best angle of fire, then Charley looked at Ewell and nodded. Ewell whipped his gun over the tree again and fired. This time he raised his head far enough to see a barrel pointing directly at him. He ducked his head an instant before the musket ball hit the tree above him. He felt a sharp pain in his head and reached up and pulled a splinter of wood out of his scalp, which was bleeding profusely.

After crawling to a new position he paused for an instant then swung his musket over the tree. He immediately saw a man in blue pointing a pistol to his right. He swung his barrel in line with him but the blood from his scalp wound was pouring into his eyes and even as he fired he knew he had missed. As he dropped behind the tree he heard two shots in rapid succession, and a scream from the Yankee position. Charlie had not missed!

The Union sergeant had suspected that the men behind the fallen tree were planning something, but Ewell's ruse had worked and he had not seen Charley change positions. To offset whatever the men were up to, he decided to change positions himself. Each time his trooper fired he moved forward a few yards until he was only about thirty yards from the fallen tree that his enemies were using for cover. When Ewell lifted his weapon over the tree a second time the sergeant was ready and probably would have killed him except that from his new position he saw Charley rise and aim at his last young trooper. But

137

Charley got his shot off, before the sergeant shot him through the middle of the chest.

The sergeant snapped off two more shots at Ewell, now safely sheltered behind his tree, as he rushed back to the aid of his trooper. As he approached the soldier's position, he knew from the way his body lay unmoving that he was dead.

Ewell reached into his pocket, pulled out a bandanna and wiped the blood from his forehead and eyes. His scalp throbbed where he had pulled out the splinter and he pressed the bloody rag against the wound to stop the bleeding. *Well*, he thought, *at least we got one of them*. He looked over to Charley's fallen tree.

At first he did not comprehend what he saw. Charley was in a kneeling position with the upper portion of his body laying over the fallen tree. He was only visible from the chest down. Ewell screamed, "Charley get down!" Charley didn't move. As he stared, Charley's left arm fell to his side and Ewell could see blood run down his wrist and drip from his fingers to the forest floor. To Ewell's horror, the dripping blood fell on the small copperhead he had seen earlier. The coiled snake struck upward biting the gently swinging hand. It was more than Ewell could bear. He screamed, "No, God No!" He tore the compress from his congealing wound and hurled it at the snake. Then he lay back and sobbed. Charley was dead!

The sergeant heard the screaming from where he sat looking at the body of his second young trooper. He had heard many men scream; in anger, in pain, in fear, and in frustration. He thought, *that's not a full-grown man*. And he began to move forward.

Ewell was alone, hot, and very afraid. All of his friends were dead. He thought, *Pa, what have I done?* He lay behind the tree for a long time. Then he said, almost aloud, *I must shoot him or he will shoot me*. He loaded his musket and each of two of his dead friends' guns and laid them next to him.

He sat back against his fallen tree, wiped the sweat from his eyes, and rested. After a while he said a prayer and cocked his musket and those of his friends. He was ready. He had three loaded muskets and once he started shooting he didn't intend to stop until he had used them all. He threw a rock into a brush pile near Charley's body, hoping to distract the Yankee momentarily. Then he flung himself upward onto one knee. Where was the Yankee? He caught a movement out of the corner of his left eye. The Yankee sergeant stepped from behind a tree, only thirty feet away! His pistol was leveled at Ewell's chest. Just for a fleeting instant Ewell thought about swinging his musket around for a shot. But he knew it was hopeless. He thought, *I'm going to die.*

This Yankee wasn't a big man, but he looked to Ewell like he had done this sort of thing before. His pistol was rock steady as he said, "Drop your musket." Ewell lowered the hammer and dropped his weapon. The sergeant lowered his pistol, but kept it at the ready. He looked at Ewell's three friends behind the fallen tree and then back at his own fallen comrades.

Ewell hadn't moved since he had dropped his musket. The sergeant looked at him with a sad expression and said, "It is a terrible thing we have done here today; what we have been doing these past three years." He holstered his pistol, reached into his pocket, took something out and placed it in Ewell's hand. Then he turned and walked slowly across the Devil's Bottom, around the curved bank of Bayberry Creek and out of sight. He never looked back.

As the Yankee walked away Ewell thought, *my musket's still loaded. I could pick it up and shoot him.* But he didn't. He couldn't.

Gradually as his shock wore off Ewell became aware of the object in his hand. It was a picture wallet. He opened it. The picture was of the big Yankee soldier. The first one to be killed that day. In the background of the picture was a farmhouse. In the foreground, the soldier stood with one arm around a woman and the other around a teenaged boy.

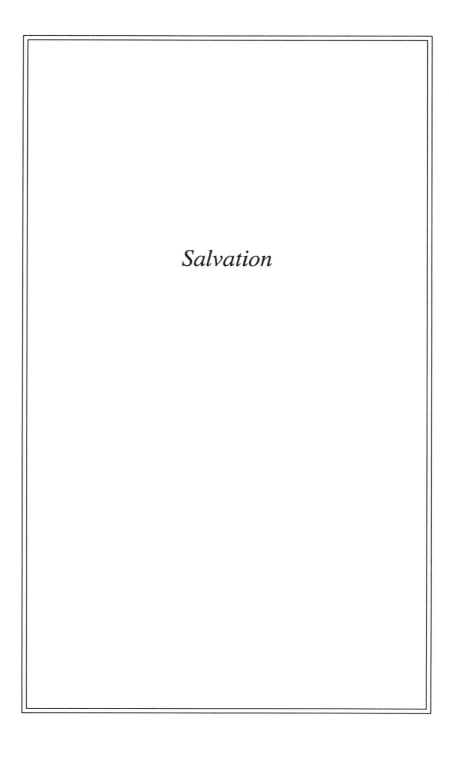

Salvation

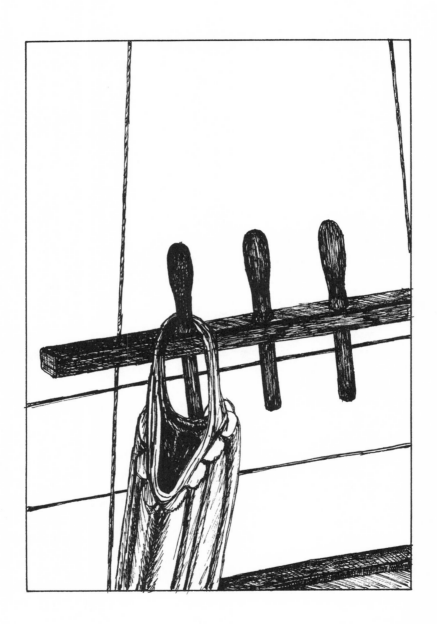

Salvation

Art knew that the storm was coming and was supposed to hit
Nassau in the early evening. He had thought that by leaving just after
sunrise that he could make Chub Cay in the Berry Islands by mid-
afternoon. The basin at Chub had been built during World War II, had
a narrow L-shaped entrance channel and would provide excellent shelter.
He had been there before and was sure he could enter it even if a heavy
sea was running.

His boat was a cutter, heavily built for offshore cruising. He had
spent a considerable amount of money upgrading and maintaining her.
His only regret was that he had not replaced her old bronze winches
with self-tailing ones. He normally sailed single-handed and without
self-tailing winches he could not keep a hand on the rudder while he
trimmed the staysail and jib. But the old winches were still in good
shape and every salesman with whom he had talked tried to overcharge
him for new ones. But that was months ago.

Art had just finished arguing with a dockmaster in Nassau over
the price of fuel that morning when the boy approached him and asked
if he was sailing to Florida and if he could use a hand. The boy said
that he had flown over to the Bahamas with friends and had lost all of
his money gambling in the casino. Trying to recoup his losses, he sold

his return plane ticket and gambled away that money as well. Now he was trying to get back to his home in the states. Art agreed to take him, not because he felt sorry for the boy, but because an extra man on the winches would lighten his load considerably. Art pretended to think about the request for a minute and then said, "We could have some heavy weather. Have you ever sailed before?" The boy nodded. "Yes sir, my father has a thirty-eight foot ketch."

He scowled at the lad. "I don't suppose you have any food in that knapsack?" The boy shook his head. Art frowned, "Well I guess you can share mine, but don't expect anything fancy. With good weather we could be in Florida in three days, but I don't know how long it will take us. You can call me Captain or Mr. Lowen. Get your things aboard. Stow them in the forward cabin, then take both anchors off the bowsprit and stow them in the empty port and starboard lockers in the main cabin. If we get into a real blow, I don't want all that extra weight up forward. By the way, what's your name?" The boy, hurrying to the forward cabin said, "Bob, my name's Bob."

While Bob struggled to remove the heavy anchors from the bowsprit, Art was tuning his amateur radio, trying to make contact with the Offshore Cruising Net. Once contact was made, he filed a float plan, giving a description of his boat, crew, current location, destination, time of departure and expected time of arrival. Then he listened to the weather forecast again. The storm was not expected to hit until after sunset. He looked to the east and saw the sun a few degrees above the horizon. Chub Cay was thirty-six nautical miles away, across the Northeast Providence Channel. With strong winds out of the northeast they should make the crossing in seven to nine hours easily. That would put them in port by mid-afternoon.

As they pulled away from the fueling dock under engine power, Art had Bob remove the sail covers. Afterward he turned the tiller over to him and checked the deck one more time. All the hatches and ports were dogged down, the boat hooks and anything else that could be carried away by a rogue wave were securely lashed to the deck. He gave Bob an old, uncomfortable life jacket and a safety harness and made sure that Bob put the jacket on over the harness. Then he ran a jackline around the deck, clipping it to the boom gallows aft and to the bowsprit forward. Now they would have something to clip their harnesses to, if they had to go up to the foredeck in heavy seas.

As they passed the red marker at the west end of Nassau Harbor and headed out into the Northeast Providence Channel, Art shut down the engine and raised the sails. He checked his watch. It was 7:05 A.M.

He looked at the watch again. His wife, Nancy, had given it to him eight months ago on his birthday; it was inexpensive but reliable. He had just retired at the time and they were living at their summer cottage on Virginia's Northern Neck, an area noted for its beautiful rivers and creeks.

Only Art called the place "the cottage." Most people who saw it called it a shack. Located several miles from the nearest body of water the cottage sat back forty to fifty feet from a dirt road among some scraggly pines. During the summer, passing cars raised clouds of dust which coated the place a dirty reddish brown. The only thing that Nancy like about the cottage was the birds. Dozens of species lived in the trees that surrounded the place and she spent many a lonely afternoon watching them and listening to their songs.

Art had bought the shack years before. He knew that someday he would buy a used sailboat from one of the boat dealers along the Rappahannock River. Used boats always needed repairs and upgrading, despite what the owners might say. To save money, he planned on doing the work himself and he knew that he couldn't commute from their home in Washington, D.C. to do it. The boat had been the dream that had kept him going as he grew to hate his job.

He had been a stock broker for thirty years. At first he had liked the work, but after a couple of years, he was getting nowhere while the friends and relatives of the boss were being promoted. To make matters worse, the better clients, those with large portfolios that generated lots of commissions, were given to these same people. Art's wife, Nancy, wasn't bothered by the fact that they didn't have much money. All she ever wanted was a home and family.

Art and Nancy started their family relatively late in life. They were both in their early thirties when they married. But within four years they had two children and had bought a house. Nancy gave up her secretarial job and became a full time mother and homemaker. Art never thought about changing jobs. He just struggled along year after year, becoming more and more bitter. Financially, Art was barely keeping his head above water. He had always wanted a sailboat but could never afford one. Occasionally he did get to crew on one of the boats of his younger, more affluent, colleagues.

He remembered his forty-fifth birthday. The day he made the decision. He thought, *to hell with everybody. From now on I'm looking out for myself first. I'm going to retire at fifty-five and go cruising.* He told Nancy, "If the kids want to go to college, they'll have to work their way through. I'm not paying." At work, he began recommending investments to his clients, not on the basis of their value, but on the size of the commission he would earn. He even lost what few friends he had by involving them in bad investments.

When Nancy could not persuade him to help the children with their college bills, she went back to work. Her skills were rusty, so she started at a low-paying clerical job. Most of her small salary went toward the childrens' college fund that she started. Art would not buy her a car, so she rode the bus. When their daughter wanted to get married, Nancy paid for the modest wedding. When the house needed repairs, it often came out of her paycheck. Art took care of his family, but in a minimal way. There were few vacations or other small events that knit a family together. He made sure that any money left at the end of the month went into his retirement fund or into a special account for the purchase of a boat.

Two weeks after his retirement in May, he found the boat he wanted to buy. The boat cost far more than the sum that he had in his special account. He told Nancy that the children were grown and that they did not need a big house in a high cost-of-living area any more. They sold the house which Nancy loved, bought the boat and moved into the cottage, all within a month's time. Then Art told Nancy of his plan.

He said that by October the boat would be ready for voyaging. They were going to sail from the Northern Neck to Florida, the Bahamas, the Virgin Islands, South America and then back. Nancy burst into tears. "I don't want to go!"

Art was ready for this response. "All right. I'll buy you a little condo in Florida, where you can stay until I return." Art didn't emphasize the word "little" when he said that he would buy Nancy a condo, but he should have, for that's what she got, a decrepit little place in one of the poorer areas of Ft. Lauderdale. His children were furious when they saw it. They hadn't talked to him since. As Art was thinking about his children, the bow of his boat plowed into a wave and the spray struck him in the face and brought him back to reality.

They were in the Providence Channel now and he knew that there was at least six thousand feet of water under the hull. The wind had picked up and it was bucking the current. The waves were four to five feet high. The sky was still a sparkling blue. He shouted to Bob, "We need to shorten sail. I'm going to bring her through the wind and backwind the jib and staysail. After that I'll go forward and reef the mainsail. When I go forward, you take the tiller and release the mainsheet when I tell you."

The operation went smoothly considering the wind and sea conditions. But reefing was hard work and when it was finished, Art was exhausted. It took him about fifteen minutes to recover his strength. The wind seemed to be slowly increasing. He looked at their wake. The water hissed as it came off the stern and seemed to boil as it faded in the distance. He turned on his small hand-held global positioning system (GPS) and recorded their position, then entered the coordinates of a point half way between Nassau and Chub Cay, and instructions that would make the instrument sound an alarm when they reached that point.

An hour later, they were still making excellent time but needed to reduce sail again, and they needed to head downwind a few more degrees. Art turned to Bob, "Furl in the Yankee jib and ease out on the staysail sheet." The Yankee jib was furled within a few minutes and shortly after the staysail sheet had been eased. The boat now sailed with a more comfortable motion.

There was a problem, however, with the self-tending staysail. The set of this sail was adjusted by a sheet in the cockpit that led to a small block and tackle system. One end of the system was shackled to the clew-end of the staysail boom and the other to a small car on a track on the cabin roof. When the boat changed tack the staysail boom flopped from one side of the boat to the other and the car slid to the same side carrying its part of the block and tackle. The car had jammed. The problem was not serious and should have been easily fixed. Art pointed at the car and said, "See that?" The boy nodded. Art told him what needed to be done. "Fasten the tether of your safety harness to the jackline and go along the port side of the deck to the track. Then jerk the car fore and aft as hard as you can. It should come loose and the staysail boom will flop out farther. Watch out for your head when the boom moves." Art had spoken slowly and loudly over the increasing noise of the wind and waves. Bob nodded again, indicating that he understood, and moved forward.

Bob did exactly as he was told. But on the first two tries the car did not come free. Art yelled, "Try again when the staysail luffs," and he headed the boat up into the wind until the sail just began to flap. The boy jerked the car. It came loose. Art headed the boat downwind again. The staysail boom flew outboard as the wind caught it. The boy's attention was riveted on the car and he did not see the boom. It missed his head by a half inch, but the block carrying the sheet to the boom hit him squarely on the right cheek, just below the eye. He was in a kneeling position when the block struck him and was knocked off the edge of the low cabin roof into the lifelines. Only his tether had prevented him from going overboard. Art lashed the tiller amidship and rushed forward.

The boy had a badly bruised cheekbone and several small cuts an inch or so below his eye. Art helped him back to the cockpit, then sent him below to put some ice on the bruise. A few minutes later he was back topside, hurting and embarrassed at his own stupidity. He looked at Art, but Art was looking at his watch.

It's noon, thought Art, *we're approaching the half-way mark. We appear to be moving through the water fast, but I think the current is moving strongly against us and I'm sure that we're not making as much speed over ground as we were earlier. The storm looks like it's going to hit sooner than predicted, but the boat seems to be handling the seas well. I don't think a more solid boat has ever been built.* At this point his mind wandered back to the day that he took possession of the boat from the previous owner.

He had driven a very hard bargain and the owner who was about to hand over the boat to him was angry. Art had approached the man several months earlier and, worming his way into his confidence, learned that he was selling the boat because he needed the money to send his daughter to college. They had verbally agreed on a price, but Art had delayed signing the papers until the start of the school year was only a few days off. Then he had told the man that he'd buy the boat only if he would lower the price, that they had previously agreed upon, by four thousand dollars.

The seller was in an untenable position and gave in. After they had finalized the deal, Art asked the man if there were any problems on the boat that he should know about. He had said, "Yes, there is one problem that could develop into something serious, but with all the money you've cheated me out of, you should have no difficulty paying a good marine surveyor to find it." Art thought, *sour grapes*. However, the next day he started at the bow of the boat and moved aft, checking every inch of it, inside and out, to see if the man was telling the truth. He found nothing seriously wrong. When he redocumented the boat, he named her *SALVATION*.

Nancy did not like the boat of course, but she did like the name. Art remembered sailing the boat down the inland waterway from

Virginia to Florida. Nancy accompanied him and she was happy as long as a shoreline was close at hand. She stayed in Ft. Lauderdale when he left for South America via the islands a few months later. He had expected to be gone about one year.

He had spent two months cruising the Bahamas when a strange thing happened. In quiet anchorages he'd hear the songs of birds carried on the evening air and remember how Nancy loved watching birds at her feeders. In small island villages he would see boating couples laughing and joking as they searched for vegetables in open air markets and a feeling of melancholy would nearly overwhelm him. After a few more weeks of this he had all he could take of the single-handed sailing life. He turned *Salvation* around and headed back to Florida. He phoned Nancy from Nassau and told her he was on his way. He was not sure how she would take the news. Now he remembered only two words of what she had said. "Hurry home." He was thinking of her when the GPS alarm sounded. They had reached the halfway point.

He looked at the boy. Bob lay stretched out on one side of the cockpit. He had taken his life jacket off, folded it and placed it under his head. He had snapped his harness tether to the port side jackline. Swelling had partially closed his eye and caused the small vertical cuts on his cheekbone to open wide. Art said, "Cheer up Bob, we're halfway there. How does the face feel?"

Bob's expression brightened a little. "It feels stiff and very sore, but a lot better than it did an hour ago. What's happening, the waves seem higher. How deep is it here?"

Art looked at the chart in the clear vinyl case beside him. "Between nine and ten thousand feet. About 1,600 fathoms. The wind is picking up, but I think it's a stronger current that's piling up the waves." Bob pondered this for a minute and then changed the subject.

"Before I laid down a few minutes ago, I saw two of the starboard shrouds jerk and vibrate a couple of times. What causes that?"

Art shook his head, "I don't know. Which two were they?" Bob pointed, "The center one and the aft one." Art gave the tiller to the boy and snapped the tether of his safety harness onto the starboard jackline.

The wind was increasing and occasionally the stern of the boat moved with a sudden corkscrew motion as they were overtaken by a wave. The sky overhead was now an ugly gray and Art had to crawl along the deck to the shrouds. They were on a broad reach and the wind was howling in from the northeast.

There were three stainless steel shrouds on this side of the boat.

The outside ones ran from chainplates bolted to the side of the hull to tangs about halfway up the mast. The center shroud went from its chainplate through the end of a spreader located halfway up the mast to a tang at the very top. Together with an identical set of shrouds on the port side, a forestay running from the bowsprit to the top of the mast, and a backstay from the stern to the top of the mast, they held the mast in a vertical position. All the rigging was oversized and the arrangement should have been immensely strong, but the shrouds were twenty years old. Grasping the two outer shrouds, Art stood upright. He jerked the shrouds violently from side to side to see if he could feel any movement in the chainplates.

Just as he jerked a second time, a powerful gust of wind struck *Salvation's* sails. At that instant the center shroud broke inside the fitting at the top of the mast, where it had been rusting, unseen, for nearly a decade. Another gust of wind hit the sails and both outer shrouds broke off inside the turnbuckle screws, where they too had nearly rusted through unnoticed.

The boat rolled sharply to port and Art, who had already lost his balance, flew across the cabin roof. Instinctively he stuck his right hand back over his head for protection. The back of his hand and his knuckles hit the main halyard winch a fraction of a second before his body smashed into the mast. He was dazed and knew that at least two of his knuckles were broken. But the worst was yet to come.

As Art lay on his back looking up the mast, a third and still heavier gust of wind hit the sails. About five feet above his head, the heavy spar bent slightly and then, unsupported by starboard shrouds, it broke. Art screamed, and rolled toward the cockpit. He thought he was about to be crushed or impaled. Instead the pull of the sails caused the mast to swing to port as it came down. The jagged end of the mast pierced the deck and then slammed into the hull below, punching a hole nearly two foot in diameter through the fiberglass. The hole was below the waterline and the sea poured in with tremendous force.

Art could not see the hole, but he heard the mast hit and felt it tear through the hull. He knew there was no way they could save the boat. And he knew they had only seconds to get off her.

Art yelled at the boy, "Get the life raft over the side!" He reached inside the hatch and grabbed the mike of his marine radio. Fortunately the radio had been mounted high on the bulkhead just inside the hatch. He held the transmit button down and looked at the face of the transceiver. The small red light, indicating that it was transmitting, glowed. He screamed "Mayday! Mayday! Mayday!" and released the mike button.

A voice responded immediately, "Identify yourself and give your location!"

Art pressed the mike button and said, "This is the......" the red light on the transceiver had gone out, the radio was dead. The water had gotten to the batteries. In the cabin, the water was already above the bunks. They had to get off the boat and into the life raft! He prayed Bob had gotten it overboard.

Bob's safety harness tether had two snap shackles on it, one at the very end which snapped onto the jackline, and one about midway along its length. The latter shackle could be snapped to the harness, effectively reducing the length of the tether by half, so that one could walk about without tripping over the tether when it was not attached to the jackline. When Bob had gone below deck to put ice on his battered cheekbone he had cinched up his safety harness tether so that he would not step on it.

The life raft was lashed to the cabin roof, just forward of the sliding hatch. Bob snapped his harness tether to the jackline and moved down the port side of the boat. The boat was wallowing as she filled with water. The knot which secured the life raft was on the opposite side of the cabin roof. As he tried to crawl across the cabin roof he was stopped by his shortened tether. He mistakenly thought it must be fouled on some object on the deck. He grabbed the tether with both hands and pulled with all of his strength.

Bob was eighteen years old and strong. Even though he was nearly crazy with fear, when it did not come free, he suddenly realized his mistake. Almost crying in frustration, he reached down and unsnapped the mid-tether shackle. He glanced over the side of the boat, the water was nearly up to the deck. He tore at the canvas that covered the life raft container. Finally it came free. Then he saw Art moving down the starboard side of the boat toward the life raft.

Art looked at him and screamed, "Get your life jacket on!" Bob struggled back to the cockpit. As he reached for the life jacket a wave broke over the back of the boat and carried the jacket away. By then Art had reached the life raft.

The slipknot that secured the raft had not been under the raft's protective canvas cover. Encrusted with salt it had not been untied in over a year and a half. He pulled at the bitter end of the rope with all the strength in his left hand, but it would not come undone. He tried his best to pry it apart with the fingers of his left hand, but the stiff line would not come free. His broken right hand was useless. Then the boat slid under. He looked for the boy.

When the boat sank, Bob had grabbed an old and worn seat cushion that was floating near him. Originally it had served as a throwable life preserver. Art had kept it to sit on even though it would no longer pass inspection for its original purpose. He saw Bob swimming toward him. Art reached out, caught him by the shoulder and yelled, "Give me your tether shackle." He held it out and Art took his own shackle and snapped the two together. The man and boy drifted apart, but they were connected by their tethers.

In the midst of the flying spray and the breaking waves, Art was having difficulty breathing without inhaling saltwater. He looked at the boy. *Salvation* had sunk only minutes before, but the cushion to which he was desperately clinging was already losing its buoyancy. Art was thinking very clearly now and he knew it was just a matter of minutes before the boy was going to drown. He called to the boy, "Put your arms through the cushion straps and pull me over to you." Bob did as he was told. Once he reached the boy Art removed his offshore life preserver and gave it him. Bob took the preserver and pushed the cushion over to Art. Resting on the sinking cushion, Art somehow found the two snap shackles that fastened the two tethers together and unsnapped them. He looked at the boy and said, "Good luck, Bob, tell my wife I loved her." He looked at the watch Nancy had given him. It was 3:30 P.M. The man and the boy drifted apart.

Both the U.S. Coast Guard and the Bahamian Air-Sea Rescue Forces had heard Art's Mayday. But having no idea where it came from, they did not know where to begin searching. The storm had hit four hours earlier than expected. It was dark by 7:00 P.M. and the storm ended in the Northeast Providence Channel by 10:00 P.M.

According to the float plan Art had filed with the Offshore Cruising Net, he was supposed to report his position at 8:00 A.M. When he did not, the net controller reported to the Coast Guard that they had a boat and crew missing somewhere between Nassau and Chub Cay. The controller provided a full description of the boat and crew. The Coast Guard began an immediate helicopter search and the Bahamian Air-Sea Rescue Force sent out boats. Nancy was notified that her husband was missing.

Six hours later a helicopter crew spotted a body floating in an offshore-type life jacket. Minutes later the body of the boy lay on the deck of the helicopter. Within an hour Art's body was found floating face down, thirteen miles off Chub Cay.

The Coast Guard commander in charge of the search conducted a thorough investigation of the accident. After taking testimony from numerous people in the islands and on the mainland who had known Art and the boy, and carefully reading the autopsy findings, he filed his report. It said, "We will never know for certain why the subject vessel sank. It was sturdy, well constructed and carried all the required safety equipment. Bruises on the hands and face of the parties involved, and conversations with persons concerning the attitudes and personality of the owner, suggests that foul play cannot be ruled out."

About the Author

Originally from Michigan, Jim Charbeneau worked most of his professional life as an analyst and manager in the Intelligence Directorate of the Central Intelligence Agency in Washington, D.C. Later, he became president of a research and writing firm specializing in the study of social issues in foreign countries. Since 1991, Mr. Charbeneau has been living on Virginia's Northern Neck. He spends much of his time sailing his boat *Mietje* on the Great Lakes, the Chesapeake Bay, the Intracoastal Waterway to Florida and the Bahamas while writing free-lance for magazines and newspapers. *Shouts and Whispers* is his first book.